Dead Sorry

ALSO BY HELEN H. DURRANT

DS HEDLEY SHARPE
Book 1: Dig Two Graves

DETECTIVE RACHEL KING
Book 1: Next Victim
Book 2: Two Victims
Book 3: Wrong Victim
Book 4: Forgotten Victim
Book 5: Last Victim
Book 6: Lost Victim

DETECTIVES CALLADINE & BAYLISS
Book 1: Dead Wrong
Book 2: Dead Silent
Book 3: Dead List
Book 4: Dead Lost
Book 5: Dead & Buried
Book 6: Dead Nasty
Book 7: Dead Jealous
Book 8: Dead Bad
Book 9: Dead Guilty
Book 10: Dead Wicked
Book 11: Dead Sorry
Book 12: Dead Real

DETECTIVE ALICE ROSSI
Book 1: The Ash Lake Murders
Book 2: The Ravenswood Murders

THE DCI GRECO BOOKS
Book 1: Dark Murder
Book 2: Dark Houses
Book 3: Dark Trade
Book 4: Dark Angel

MATT BRINDLE
Book 1: His Third Victim
Book 2: The Other Victim

DETECTIVES LENNOX & WILDE
Book 1: The Guilty Man
Book 2: The Faceless Man
Book 3: The Wrong Woman

Helen H. Durrant

DEAD SORRY

Detectives Calladine & Bayliss Book 11

JOFFE BOOKS

Revised edition 2025
Joffe Books, London
www.joffebooks.com

First published in Great Britain in 2021

This paperback edition was first published
in Great Britain in 2025

Cover art by Nick Castle

ISBN: 978-1-80573-037-8

PROLOGUE

Twenty-five years ago

It was her own fault. She should have made some excuse, told them not to come. But she hadn't, and now she was paying the price.

Make friends, her granny said, invite a few classmates back after school, try and fit in. But she doesn't fit, does she, and that's the problem. Millie is different from them. She doesn't swear or drink, and she works hard at school. So they point and sneer and call her "teacher's pet". Little do they know.

Jade, the ringleader, grabs her round the throat. Millie pushes her hand away and steps back. The girl merely grins. "What d'you keep in that shed thing outside?"

"It's not a shed, it was my granddad's workshop." Millie is terrified. She knows this will have a bad outcome.

"Show me."

Jade grabs her hair and yanks her towards the back door. "I'm after tools Johnno can sell. He makes a bob or two and we'll have a good night."

As Millie knows, Jade lives with her druggie mother in a hovel of a flat on the Hobfield, and Johnno is a dealer. "There's . . . there's not much," she says.

1

"Better be something worth the effort or you'll suffer." Jade beckons the others to follow. "You're full of shit, d'you know that? A weirdo who needs a lesson in manners. What d'you reckon, Kaz? Should we have some fun, show her who's boss?"

Kaz says nothing. She and a third girl, Sarah, just follow in Jade's wake, their faces still buried in a magazine Kaz had found in the sitting room.

"Look, you should go. My granny's back soon, and this is just a waste of time," Millie says as they cross the yard.

"Shut it!" Jade says.

They enter the shed and Jade flicks the light on. "Right. Power tools — what've you got?"

"I told you, nothing."

Jade picks up a drill from the bench. "Lying bitch. That'll cost you," she says, spitting out the words. "Johnno'll get a few quid for this beauty for a start." She tosses the thing over to Sarah. "I'll take this, too." She hefts a metal box containing an assortment of tools. "You lied, Millie, and I hate liars." Her wicked smile sends shivers down the girl's spine.

This really wasn't going to end well. "Get out!" Millie shouts. "You've got what you wanted. Now leave me alone."

"Make us," Jade taunts, pushing her face into the other girl's. "Go on, lying cow, show us what you're made of." As Jade's hand moves, Millie spots the metallic glint of a Stanley knife. She's picked it up from the bench and is now wielding it in front of the terrified girl's face. She turns to the others. "Watch. I'm going to cut her. That stupid mole on her face will be the first thing to go. I'm going to scar the bitch for life. But first I'm having this little beauty." Jade snatches the gold locket that's hanging around Millie's neck before lashing out and slicing into her cheek.

"No!" Millie's hands fly to her face, she looks at them and they're covered in blood. "You'll get into trouble now. You don't want that, do you? Better if you just go."

Jade laughs, thrusting the blade within a spit of the girl's other cheek. "I can make a right mess with this. Everyone who

2

looks at you will feel sick." She nudged her friend. "Watch this, Kaz. I'm going to cut her again. She's so scared she won't lift a finger to stop me."

But she's wrong. Jade has no idea. Millie is scared all right, but not of Jade. She's given them every chance, politely asked them to stop, but still the torment has continued. Well, it will end now, and it won't be pretty.

Millie feels the familiar rage boil up through her body and screams as the frenzy takes hold.

* * *

What took place after that, Millie could not recall exactly, try as she might. But one thing that remained imprinted on her mind's eye was the look of utter disbelief on Jade's face as the lump hammer hit the side of her head. A split second later, Jade fell like a stone to the floor. Next, she went for Kaz, slamming the hammer into her head too. Sarah stood stock-still for a second and then ran for her life. Millie heard Jade groan. So she wasn't dead. Pity. She would've put that right, but the familiar, loving voice brought her back to the moment.

Her granny was home. Millie closed her eyes and repeated the comforting words, the ones that always got her through.

It'll be all right. Granny knows what to do.

"I had no choice, it was me or them," she whimpered, watching Jade crawl towards the door. Millie saw the shock on her granny's face as she looked at Kaz struggling to get to her knees. "There's another one but she ran away," she said. "They'll tell the police. Sarah saw everything. They'll take me away from you!"

Granny shook her head. "You lost it again. I warned you, Millie. I told you to be careful." She held the girl close. "And your poor face. We'll have to see to that before it gets infected." She looked around the shed at the mess, ignoring Jade and Kaz who were holding each other up as they made their way out of the door and towards the third girl waiting for them behind a clump of trees. "This is bad. There will be questions. We must make sure no one finds out the truth." She handed Millie a hanky. "Wipe the blood from your face, then take your satchel and go. Walk around the hill and come back up the path. I'll clear up here." She hugged Millie close. "Let those girls go, let them tell the police their tales. If they come here, I promise you they won't find a thing. All they'll see is you returning home from school. This will be our secret, child. You, me and Gorse House will hide this mess for ever."

CHAPTER 1

The present day

Day One

Tom Calladine handed the wriggling infant back to his daughter, Zoe. "I'll just sort this and we'll get back. We don't want the little one getting cold." He hunkered down and brushed away the twigs and fallen leaves littering his mother's grave in Leesdon churchyard. He replaced the dying flowers in the vase with a bunch of fresh ones, stood back and smiled. "Yellow roses, her favourites." Glancing up, he noted dark clouds gathering over the hills in the distance. The weather was closing in. Late autumn. There'd be snow up on the tops before long.

"Freda Jean." Zoe kissed one of her baby girl's soft pink cheeks and pointed to the headstone. "Your great-granny."

"Freda would have loved this, seeing the family grow, knowing she had a stake in the future."

"I'm glad I met her, Dad. We didn't know each other well but I liked her a lot," Zoe said.

"She liked you too," he said softly.

She nodded at the grave alongside Freda's. "You don't say much about your dad though. You don't hold what he did against him, do you?"

Did he? Calladine had never given it much thought. "If anyone was upset by what happened, it should have been Freda. I mean, he had an affair. Good job he did, or I wouldn't be here. And it just shows the sort of woman Freda was to take on her husband's love child and raise me as her own."

Zoe laughed. "I've never thought of you as a 'love child'. Come to think of it, you never say much about either of your parents. You must have tales to tell. I'd like to hear them sometime."

"I've got boxes of old photos at home. I'll bring them round one night. Freda was quite a looker in her day, you know."

"I've often heard people refer to her as 'Jean'. Didn't she like the name Freda?" Zoe asked.

"She didn't mind either, it depended on who she was talking to. That waster of a cousin of mine, Ray Fallon, used to call her Auntie Jeannie. Thought it was less old-fashioned. Speaking of names, what about the child? Come up with anything you like yet? You're running out of time to register the birth."

Zoe rolled her eyes. "Try telling Julian that. Truth is, Dad, we just can't agree, but like you say, we've only got a few days left and then we're in trouble."

"A family name perhaps?" he suggested.

Ignoring that suggestion, Zoe said, "What d'you think about Maisie?"

"Maisie Calladine. Hmm, got a nice ring to it, and unusual. You don't get many Maisies in Leesdon."

"Exactly. You have no objections?"

"Not my place, is it?" Calladine smiled. "Let's get both of you home. Poor little thing's getting grizzly."

"And it'll be Maisie Brandon Calladine," Zoe said firmly. "Can't leave Jo out, she's feeling sidelined enough."

"Why?"

"Julian's the biological father, I gave birth to her. Jo feels a bit surplus at times, I know."

"You'll have to put her right," he said. "The pair of you are Maisie's parents — it's what was agreed. Julian will just have to accept that."

"I hope so."

Calladine smiled. "But the surname is a bit of a mouthful."

"She'll grow into it," Zoe said firmly. "Let's get gone, it's bloody freezing out here. There's a mug of hot coffee waiting when we get back, and you can look at all the prezzies we've been given." Zoe Calladine secured her daughter in the car seat and climbed in beside her. "It's embarrassing — there's enough baby stuff there to kit out a shop."

"Is Jo okay with Maisie?" Calladine asked.

"Almost. I'm slowly winning the battle." Zoe grinned. "Julian, though, is another matter. He wants us to call her Julia, you know, a feminine version of his own name."

"You know what he's like."

She laughed. "A first-class pain in the neck."

It took them only ten minutes to reach the house in Lowermill where Zoe and her partner, Jo Brandon, lived. Calladine parked up and carried the sleeping infant, still strapped in her car seat, up the front steps.

Inside, Zoe gestured at the pile of baby goods in the sitting room. "Just look at all this. Apart from the useful stuff, there's loads of toys she'll never play with. Jo suggested we give some to the local tots group."

"Not a bad idea. Let's have that coffee, then I'll leave you in peace. You're looking a bit ragged around the edges. You should get your feet up while she's asleep."

"Thanks a million, Dad, right confidence booster you are. But you're right, sleep is a problem. We're neither of us getting much. That little madam might look all cute and innocent, but you should hear the racket she makes in the middle of the night."

Zoe disappeared into the kitchen to sort the coffee, leaving Calladine to look at the presents. Arrayed on top of a chest of drawers was a pile of clothing, along with soft toys, some still in boxes.

"We've had loads from people you know," Zoe told him. "Some of them must have been pricey, too. That large pink teddy with the gold bow, for instance, is sporting a designer label. Came special delivery a couple of days back."

"You must never forget I know some nice people, but I also know a helluva lot of not so nice ones. You should be careful what you accept."

"It's a toy, Dad, what d'you think it's going to do, explode?"

He picked up the box. He supposed he was being a bit over-dramatic — until he read the card: *For the child, regards, Lazarov.*

Calladine felt his stomach knot. A few months back, a Bulgarian gangster called Andrei Lazarov had sworn to do him harm. The man was a known killer and — despite police efforts to catch him — still free.

"Can I take this?" He saw the look on Zoe's face, she obviously thought he was overdoing the safety angle.

"If you must, but I really like that one, the fur is gorgeous, so plush. What possible use can it be to you, Dad?"

"The man who sent it to you wants me dead," he said simply.

CHAPTER 2

Having looked at the other gifts Zoe had received for the infant, Calladine left for the station via the Duggan Centre. The child's biological father, Professor Julian Batho, was the senior forensic scientist there. Calladine wanted the expensive teddy bear gone over with a fine-tooth comb. The problem was, should he involve Julian or not? The man was so wrapped up in his role as new father that if he thought the child was in danger, he'd never leave her side, which would do Zoe's head in. Calladine decided to compromise and leave the toy with Roxy Atkins. Granted, she was in IT forensics, but prior to that she'd worked with Julian and knew the ropes. Even more important, she knew when to keep her mouth shut.

The outing with Zoe and the detour to the Duggan meant he didn't get to Leesdon station until lunchtime. He was hoping for a quiet lunch in the canteen, but before he had time to order, Ruth Bayliss, his sergeant and close friend, collared him.

"Enjoy your time with the little one?" she asked, putting her coat on. "Where did proud granddaddy take her then?"

"Leesdon churchyard," he replied. "The three of us visited Freda's grave."

Ruth snorted. "Bet the poor little thing loved that! Honestly, Tom, you've no idea. A bloody graveyard, for goodness' sake. What's wrong with the park or feeding the ducks like other granddads?"

"Thought she'd like to meet the ancestors. Anyway, it was Zoe's idea. It was Freda's birthday last week and she wanted to take some fresh flowers. Have I missed much? Where are you off to?"

"We've had an anonymous call about an incident on the Hobfield. The caller didn't give much detail, simply that there'd been an accident and we'd find a body in number sixty-seven Heron House. Life in our little neck of the woods doesn't get any easier, does it?"

"Legit, d'you reckon?"

Ruth shrugged. "Might be, or it could be a hoax, but we can't take the chance."

"Okay, you go ahead, and I'll join you in a while. I need a quick word with Greco first. If there is a body and you suspect foul play, get Natasha on it at once."

"I do know my job, Tom."

Calladine wanted to speak to Greco about Lazarov, ask if anything was known about his current activities. Stephen Greco was Leesdon's DCI, newly promoted from Oldston station. He and Calladine had history, the relationship hadn't started well. But the new dispensation dictated that both had to try harder and make it work, Calladine in particular.

Greco was at his desk, elbow deep in paperwork, when Calladine entered his office. For once, the usually impeccably dressed DCI had his jacket off and his shirtsleeves rolled up. "What is it, Tom?" he asked, looking annoyed at the interruption. "They want this lot sorted by five. Promotion! Huh. I've become nothing more than a glorified office boy."

Exactly how Calladine had felt when he'd done the job on a temporary basis. He smiled to himself. How long would Greco keep this up before he threw in the towel? At least all the papers were in neat piles and he was sifting through them in some sort of order. Calladine had never admitted it but when he'd been behind that desk, he'd binned a fair amount. "My new granddaughter has received a gift from Lazarov, a flash teddy in a box."

Greco's head shot up and he stared at Calladine. "Andrei Lazarov? Are you sure?"

"Yes. Made my heart miss a beat, I can tell you. Do we know anything about what he's up to these days?"

Greco's eyes narrowed. "I've not had any intel. He was living with his mother on the outskirts of Huddersfield, but he's not been there for a while. I know the West Yorkshire force are still looking for him, but without success. D'you think the gift could be a hoax?" he asked.

"From someone else, you mean? Who knows?" Calladine said. "But if it's genuine, it means the villain knows about my private life, down to the fact that I'm now a grandfather. That smacks of research, and I worry that he's planning something nasty."

"Like I said, it could be someone winding you up," Greco suggested. "When Lazarov slipped through the net, the grapevine had him back in Bulgaria and nothing's been heard since. But there's bound to be members of his gang still lurking in our neck of the woods. Perhaps one of them is to blame?"

"All I know, Stephen, is that the man is evil, and he holds me responsible for the collapse of his many lucrative activities around here. He lost a lot of money, and in Lazarov's eyes that means I owe him. Doesn't make for a quiet night's sleep, I can tell you.

"What have you done with the toy?" Greco asked.

"I've given it to Roxy to examine properly. You know Julian. If he finds out, he'll go ballistic and not leave the baby's side."

"We'll see what Dr Atkins finds first, and if the toy is in any way dangerous we'll think again," Greco said. "Meanwhile, I'll look out for any intel that's floating around."

Seemed reasonable enough. But in the meantime, Calladine would make his own arrangements. He'd never forgive himself if the job and the villains he dealt with were to harm his family.

* * *

Calladine pulled into the Hobfield estate and parked up. Two ageing tower blocks loomed above him like twin portents of doom. He hated this place. As far back as he could remember, nothing good had come out of the Hobfield. In one way or another, most of the cases he dealt with involved this estate and he was growing weary of it. He just hoped that whatever was waiting for him wasn't bad enough to turn his stomach. To make matters worse, the lift was broken as usual, so he had to trudge up six flights of stone stairs.

"It's definitely murder," Ruth told Calladine as soon as he arrived, panting, on the sixth-floor deck of Heron House. "A frenzied attack, Natasha reckons. The poor woman's been beaten to death. The blow that did it smashed her skull in so that you can see the brain."

Calladine was still gasping for breath. "Just what we need," he wheezed. "Any initial ideas? A drug deal gone wrong perhaps?"

"We'll soon know. Natasha and Julian are looking at the flat now." Ruth looked him up and down. "You don't look too clever. What's going on?"

"Just something with Zoe, nothing important." Calladine didn't want to discuss the toy or his fears just yet, not even with Ruth, and anyway, Julian could appear at any moment. As Greco had suggested, they'd wait for Roxy's results.

"Never mind Zoe, I'm talking about the grey tinge to your face and the fact that you're totally out of breath."

"I'm just tired," he said. Which wasn't a lie. He had been feeling fragile recently, nothing he could find a reason for, so he put it down to age.

"You should take a holiday. You haven't been away in years," she said.

"I'm fine, and who wants a holiday at this time of year? Anyway, I've no one to take."

"You don't need anyone," Ruth said. "You could go abroad, a cruise or something. You'd have a great time, a man on his own. You'd have women flocking round you."

Calladine shook his head. "I've promised Zoe I'll give her a hand with the little one. She and Jo are splitting the maternity leave so they can keep the businesses going. I'll step in on the days they're both tied up."

"They're young women, they've got tons more energy than you. Anyway, what d'you know about running an estate agent's or being a solicitor? My advice — leave them to it. You look as if you need all the rest you can get."

"I can look after the little one, answer the phone and take messages. I'm not useless, you know, and I've told you, I'm fine."

"You're still breathless."

"Six flights of stairs will do that."

"You should get yourself checked out. Why not have a word with Doc Hoyle?" Ruth suggested.

"The doc is a busy man. He won't want me banging on about a bit of breathlessness."

Ruth gave him one of her unimpressed looks. "I'd give the childminding duties another thought if I were you."

"But I want to be involved," he insisted. "I missed out on Zoe, didn't even know she existed. Little Maisie gives me a second chance."

"Is that her name then?"

"Zoe likes it, but not a word to Julian."

CHAPTER 3

They'd had a quiet few weeks but Calladine, ever the realist, had known it wouldn't last. Now it looked as if the days of keeping office hours and getting home in time for tea were finally over.

The sight that greeted him as he stood in the doorway of the flat was truly awful. The woman lay on the lino, limbs splayed at unnatural angles. It didn't take much medical knowledge to know they were broken. Her face was fast disappearing under the close attention of dozens of maggots, and brain tissue gaped from a hole in her skull. "Do we know her?"

"No, and neither do the neighbours, or if they do, they're not saying," Ruth replied.

Typical Hobfield. Do nothing, say nothing — and particularly not to the police.

They both pulled on the coveralls one of Natasha's team handed to them and went to take a look. They hesitated in the open doorway before going in. The smell coming from the flat was revolting.

Dr Natasha Barrington, the Home Office pathologist from the Duggan, was kneeling by the body. "She's been here a while."

"That smell — it's making me feel sick," Calladine said.

"That's not like you," Ruth said, nudging him.

"Someone left the heating on high," Natasha said. "It might have been deliberate to accelerate decomposition and muddy the waters forensically, and it's certainly not helped."

Calladine took a few steps forward. The victim was lying on her back. He shuddered. "Why all the maggots?"

"She vomited shortly before death, there's some still in her mouth, it attracted the flies."

"Poor bugger, left here to rot. Surely someone in this godforsaken place must have noticed the smell," he said.

"This is the Hobfield, Tom. You expect too much," Ruth said.

"There's a lot of blood around the head where she hit the ground. Most of it has dried on the floor, and there are splatters over that wall." Natasha pointed them out.

"There must have been a fight of sorts," Ruth said. "She'd at least have struggled. It would have taken time. The killer didn't stop at one blow either. From the look of the body, they went on and on. Someone along this deck must have heard something."

"Ruth is right," Natasha said. "She has multiple broken bones. Poor woman. She took some beating." She pointed. "And then there's that over there."

They'd been so intent on the body, and the state of it, that they hadn't seen what was on the bare wall nearest the body. The single word, *sorry*, and a small drawing, both written in blood. The drawing was indistinct. They took a closer look.

"What d'you make of that?" Calladine asked.

"Well, it's interesting. It's just not consistent with what went on," Ruth said. "From the look of the body, they hit her over and over, so when, I wonder, did they decide they were sorry?"

Ruth had a point. "Whoever did this must have been covered in blood," Calladine said. He went to the door and looked up and down the deck. "Someone must have heard or seen something. Do we have names for the folk who live along here?"

"Not yet, but we'll do some digging," Ruth said. "They won't speak to us though. If this is drug-related they'll see it as more than their lives are worth."

Natasha looked up from the body. "There's nothing on her, no mobile or bag. The flat is empty except for a sofa and that old mattress in the corner. It looks to me as if she was dossing down in here."

"Perhaps she was, but she'll have left the flat, even if only to score drugs." The woman was skinny, like so many other drug users they'd seen over the years. "I'll take a wander up the deck, see if anyone will at least tell us who she is. A name would make our job easier," Calladine said, happy for an excuse to be out of the stifling flat.

He knocked on the door of the neighbouring flat. A woman with an infant tucked under her arm stood glaring at him defiantly.

"What now?" she demanded. "Noisy lot, aren't you? You've woken the little mite here."

"Sorry," Calladine said. "Did you know the woman next door?"

"Nope. Saw her once, nasty piece of work. Heard her though, playing that bleeding music at all hours of the night. Off her head most of the time. I'm not surprised she's dead." She narrowed her eyes and looked at him. "Overdose, was it?"

"We're still investigating," Calladine said. "Was there anyone living with her?"

"A bloke came and visited, sometimes he stayed."

"Does he have a name?"

"No idea who he is," she said.

"When did you hear her last?" Calladine asked.

"Three or four nights ago. It's been like the grave since, so we all got some peace. She wasn't even supposed to be there, a squatter she was. The family who lived in that flat left months ago, couldn't find the rent."

In Calladine's opinion, asking people to find rent for one of these was an insult. The two blocks were old and poorly maintained. He knocked at doors a little further on but no one else responded. The neighbours were either out or just not answering, probably the latter. Three or four days ago was all he had until Natasha got to work. That would have to do for time of death.

"Woman next door said she hasn't heard her these last few nights," he said to Natasha.

"I need to get her on the slab, but that could be right, Tom, given the state of the body. You'll have more just as soon as I've done some tests and analysed the insect life in those wounds on her face."

Calladine saw Ruth shudder. Death still got to her — well, she was lucky. The older he got, the more cynical he became and, apart from the smell, the less such scenes bothered him.

"Rocco is joining us," she said. "I'll hang around, we'll talk to a few more of the tenants, see what we can find out about our victim."

Calladine nodded. "Get the names of everyone who lives on this deck. The neighbour said she played loud music every night."

"Probably on her mobile, though we haven't found one."

"I'll head back to the station, get Alice on the missing persons file."

"PM in the morning!" Natasha called out to his retreating back.

"We'll be there," he said with a cheery wave.

He made his way down the stairs to his car. It was way past lunchtime and he'd only had a coffee for breakfast. The canteen would be his first stop as soon as he got back. He'd just started the engine and pulled out when there was a loud crash and his car slewed sideways.

CHAPTER 4

A woman ran towards him, looked at the damage to the front left wing of Calladine's vehicle and gasped. "I'm so sorry," she said. "I just didn't see you. Are you all right?"

Calladine got out and examined his broken headlight and the scuff marks on the paintwork. The local garage would fix the light, they owed him a favour. As for the paintwork, he wasn't really bothered. The car was old and not worth much. "I'm fine, there's no need to panic," he told the woman. "The car was hardly in the best nick in the first place. D'you want to take a minute?"

She shook her head. "I can't, I've got to get back to work." She looked up at him. "How d'you want to play this? Insurance, or what?"

"Whatever you want is fine by me. Is there much damage to your vehicle?"

"My bumper got a tiny dent, that's all." She gave him a half-hearted smile. "I'm more bothered about yours."

"Well, don't be, I'll get it fixed myself."

She rummaged in her bag and produced a card. "You must let me pay, please, I insist. It'll make me feel so much better."

Calladine looked at the card. Her name was Kitty Lake. She was manager of a restaurant and bar in Lowermill, Mother's Kitchen. So, she was local. He'd never seen her before. "You really don't have to, there's no need to feel obligated. This old heap needs trading in anyway." He smiled. "I've just held on to it because I'm too lazy."

Kitty Lake smiled. She gave a loud sigh of relief. "Thanks for taking it this way. There are plenty who'd jump down my throat and demand a full respray at the very least."

"Not me. I need my car for work, it's not a status symbol." The woman was well dressed, and her car was an expensive model. She was definitely out of place on the Hobfield. "What are you doing round here anyway?"

"I got lost. I turned into the estate intending to park up and get my bearings," she said.

Calladine shook his head. "This estate is no place to hang around, believe me. Park for any length of time and the toerags will have your wheels."

She looked doubtful.

"I'm not joking," Calladine said. "The Hobfield is a dangerous place."

"I haven't lived around here long, I'm not familiar with the dodgy places yet," she said.

"Well, remember this one."

"You won't let me pay, and we're not involving the insurance companies, I'm really grateful. Having to go through them would really have stitched up my no-claims. Why are you being so reasonable? The car's not stolen, is it? You've just said this is a dodgy place."

Calladine gave a laugh. "God, no. Who'd want to pinch this heap? Besides, I'm a policeman. I assure you there's nothing dodgy going on."

This made Kitty Lake laugh too. "Okay, Mr Policeman. Well, perhaps you'll let me take you out to dinner instead," she said. "Only if you want to, of course, and if there isn't a Mrs Policeman."

Well, why not? There was no woman in his life currently and she was very attractive. "I'm single and my name's Tom, Tom Calladine, and I'd love to have dinner with you sometime."

"Tonight?"

Calladine hesitated. They had a murder on their hands and there was work to do.

"Even policemen have to eat," she said. "We can go to my restaurant, 'Mother's Kitchen'. It's a nice place, good wholesome northern food. You'll enjoy it."

"Not so nice that have I to dress up too much, I hope," he said.

"No, it's not that special. Wear what you want."

Calladine knew the one she meant. On Lowermill High Street, it had only recently opened. He nodded. "Okay, it's a date. Shall we say eight and meet inside?"

"Thank you, you've eased my conscience no end. I feel tons better now."

He watched her drive off. She was younger than him, slender, and her long dark hair blew about her face charmingly. As for him . . . Calladine shook his head. He preferred not to think about how much he'd gone downhill of late. He wasn't sure that the invitation was anything more than Kitty easing her guilty conscience. In any other circumstances, she wouldn't have looked twice at him.

Calladine looked up and saw Ruth watching from the sixth-floor balcony. As soon as Kitty Lake took off in her car, she rang his mobile.

"Can't leave you alone for five minutes, can I? Who is she?" Ruth asked.

Calladine looked at the card again. "Kitty Lake. She manages a restaurant in Lowermill and she pranged my car."

"So why all the smiles?"

"Because we've come to an arrangement. No insurance and I won't let her pay, so she's taking me out to dinner." He beamed up at her.

"You amaze me. A pretty face, and common sense flies out the window."

"I'm surprised you could see her from up there. You're right though, she is a bit of looker. Dinner will be no hardship at all."

Calladine gave Ruth a wave and drove off. He felt better, more positive. Meeting Kitty Lake had been just the boost he needed.

CHAPTER 5

Back at the station, Calladine grabbed a pack of sandwiches and a coffee in the canteen and went upstairs to his office. He found a message from Roxy on his mobile. She needed a word.

He rang her straight away. Maybe she had something on the toy he'd left with her.

"I took it apart and examined it thoroughly. There's nothing, Tom. The toy is fine, it poses no danger at all. I've even managed to stitch it back together. It's as good as new, so you can pick it up when you come in for the PM tomorrow."

Well, that was a huge relief. But his instincts told him that if it had really come from Lazarov, he hadn't sent the toy for no reason. It had to be a warning. "Thanks, Roxy, I owe you. I still haven't decided whether to tell Julian."

"Your decision. He doesn't know what I've been up to since yesterday."

"Okay. For now, let's keep it that way."

Calladine decided to give Greco an update and see if he had any new information. Greco was at his desk as usual. How he managed this aspect of the job puzzled Calladine. The man had been an excellent detective and, as far as he was aware, had liked the day-to-day detective work. Deskwork was the price he had to pay for the Grace debacle, he supposed.

He told Greco about Roxy's findings.

"Good, but you'll have to tell your daughter to be on her guard, Tom," Greco said firmly. "On the plus side, I've spoken to our colleagues in Huddersfield, and they are unaware of any activity by him or his gang since the time we encountered him."

"That means nothing, the man has plenty of others to do his dirty work. Lazarov is a seasoned villain."

"What action d'you want to take?" Greco asked.

"The gift is a threat, Lazarov showing me how easy it would be to harm those I love. I have no choice but to accept that my family is in danger. Having a new baby makes Zoe vulnerable. A threat against her presses all the right buttons as far as I'm concerned."

Greco nodded. "I understand. I'd feel the same in your shoes."

"If this is down to Lazarov, I doubt he'll leave things as they are. I expect there will be other attempts," Calladine said soberly.

"Okay, we won't take any risks. I'll appoint a family liaison officer to the case," Greco said.

Calladine didn't argue. It would ease his mind to know there was someone with Zoe, closely watching what went on. "D'you have anyone in mind?"

"Yes, Amanda Knight. She's an excellent officer. We need to get this organized quickly. She'll work unobtrusively, perhaps undercover within your daughter's business, and I want her to start immediately."

"Thanks, Stephen. That takes the pressure off."

Back in his office, Calladine called Zoe on his mobile. She answered in a whisper.

"I've just got her off. What is it?"

She sounded tired. He didn't want to burden her with this, but what choice did he have? "That toy, I've had it checked and it's fine. But make no mistake, it was a warning, and I doubt it'll be the last. If you or, heaven forbid, Maisie was to be injured because of me, I'd never forgive myself. Be careful, Zoe, anything else comes from Lazarov, put it in the garage and call me."

"Why would anyone want to harm an infant, Dad?"

"It's me he's getting at, not you. Just be careful and tell Jo as well. I haven't said anything to Julian. I'm still debating that one."

"He'll flip. I can see his reaction now. Leave it, please."

"There is something else. We're getting you some protection, a family liaison officer called Amanda Knight. You have plenty of room so I suggest she stays with you. You can tell anyone who asks that she's a friend come to help out with the businesses while you and Jo get used to being new parents. Her job is to see and hear things you and Jo might miss. She knows what to look out for. She'll also keep you posted with events."

"Isn't that taking things a bit far, Dad? I'm not sure about this. Is it absolutely necessary? Julian is bound to ask questions, what do I tell him?"

"Julian won't know her. Like I said, tell him she's a friend, and that you're taking time off to be with Maisie. I want you to accept this, Zoe. I need to know you have someone with you who knows the ropes."

Zoe was sensible. When she thought it through, she'd see he was right.

"Okay, I'll give her the spare room. I just hope she likes newborns, that's all."

"I'll see you in the morning. Any problems, ring me."

The FLO was more for his own peace of mind than Zoe's. She wouldn't appreciate the danger. He'd give it a week or so and see what happened. If there were any more gifts or incidents he wasn't happy with, Calladine would make his own arrangements. Above all else, he needed to know that Zoe and her family were safe. Calladine had a long-standing friend, Ronnie Merrick, who used to be a security officer with one of the large banks in Manchester. These days, apart from a little private investigating, he was practically retired, but he was still able to handle himself. Calladine decided to ring him later and put him on standby.

CHAPTER 6

Mother's Kitchen was busy for a weeknight. Well placed on Lowermill High Street, it appeared, when Calladine stepped inside, to be the preserve of young, up-and-coming business types. For several minutes, he hung around in the entrance feeling decidedly out of place. He scanned the room and saw Kitty Lake at the bar. She beckoned to him.

She smiled. "Mr Policeman, I did wonder if you'd come. I mean, I prang your car and then have the cheek to ask you out as recompense."

"The car is old, and it's been pranged many times before," he said.

"I'm forgiven, then?" she asked demurely. "I would like us to be friends. I'm new to the area and so far I've hardly met anyone."

An offer the bemused Calladine couldn't refuse. He still didn't understand why this attractive, expensively dressed younger woman would want to know him at all.

She smiled. "I've booked us a table for half eight. I thought you might like a drink first."

Calladine nodded. "A beer, please," he said to the barman. "I've not been here before. When did you open? It can't have been long ago."

"Oh, it's not my business," she said hastily. "I merely manage the place, but I am enjoying it. I've been here about a month. The owner will open another one in Hopecross if this does well. If that happens, I'm hoping he offers me a partnership. I'm ready for a new venture."

Calladine grinned. "Ambitious women scare the hell out of me."

"I'm not that scary, believe me. I'm just trying hard to make friends locally and fit in."

"Apart from me, who else have you met?" he asked.

"Ronan next door has been very helpful. Ronan Sinclair, the curator of the museum."

"I don't think I know him."

"He's been a godsend. He's allowed me to leave a bunch of leaflets for the restaurant in the museum reception area. If this business is to take off, I need to get the locals in, make it a regular haunt."

Calladine cast his eyes around the stylish interior. "If I remember rightly, this building used to be the old bank."

"Yes, then it became a small market with various outlets and now this. It's had a complete refurb, and it's worked too, we're attracting the kind of customers we want."

"That include me?" he asked. "Looking at your clientele, I definitely don't fit the profile."

Kitty laughed, shook her head. "You fit in fine."

"Now I know you're lying. I'm not young or trendy enough for starters. Look at them in here." He nodded to a table of young twenty-somethings, all in smart suits with preened hair. "There's no way an old fogey like me fits in."

"This lot here tonight are Ronan's doing. He suggested I offer vouchers for cut-price drinks to selected businesses and addresses in the Leesworth area. They've come along for a nosey, but I can't see them becoming regulars."

"Selected. I see. Sinclair suggested you target those people he reckons have money."

"Something like that," she said with another smile. "Like I said, he's a godsend, and he knows his stuff. He's full of bright ideas and keen to see the venture work so that I get the opportunity to invest and change my life."

Calladine rolled his eyes. Keen to get close to Kitty more like.

She tapped his arm and put a finger to her lips. "D'you see that woman at the corner table, the one with the young man hanging on her every word?"

Calladine glanced across. The woman was about forty, dark-haired and wearing a suit. She did look vaguely familiar.

"It's Gloria Golding, the restaurant critic. Another of Ronan's ideas, but one I could do without. She's a personal friend of his, apparently. I must say, having her here tonight, poring over our offerings, isn't doing my nerves any good."

Calladine looked again. So that's why she seemed familiar, he'd seen her on the box. "You're hoping for a good write-up then?"

"We're relying on it, Tom. She tells the world we serve up rubbish and we sink like a stone. That woman is ruthless. She's eaten her way through most of the Manchester restaurants and rubbished at least half of them."

"I'd no idea this business was so cut-throat."

"Well, now you do. I guess all we can do is serve up our best and keep everything crossed."

"If he's so ambitious, why did the owner choose to bury the place in a backwater like Lowermill? Surely the money to set up this and the one in Hopecross would have been more than enough to start up in the city, the Northern Quarter in Manchester for instance. Eateries and wine bars do really well there, I'm told."

"He wasn't keen, and neither was I. I've put in enough years working amid the hustle and bustle of the city and I needed a change. The countryside suits me better." She nodded towards the dark, shadowy hills in the distance. "I don't recall much about it, but my mother used to take me on picnics up there when I was a kid. We'd get the train from Manchester and make a day of it. Even then I loved the village atmosphere, the narrow streets and stone houses. When I got the opportunity to run this place, I just had to take it."

"Have you got somewhere to live?"

"I'm dossing in the flat upstairs for the time being, but I'm in the market for a property. I want the perfect place, a stone cottage by the canal. Somewhere quiet and quaint, but I wouldn't mind moving up there if something came up." She nodded towards the hills.

Calladine laughed. "Don't be taken in by the quaint old villages round here, because it's not that quiet, believe me. You can find it up in the hills, but a word of warning, some properties up there don't even have a full set of utilities." He grinned. "I could take you now to a cottage that's still lit by gas."

She laughed. "I'm not sure I want to take the rural life that far. A beam or two, an inglenook fireplace, but I do need mod cons."

"My daughter's partner is an estate agent, the one along the High Street. Go and see Jo, mention my name and I'm sure she'll do a good job for you."

"Actually, I have seen somewhere, and not far from here, just along the canal."

"Canalside Cottages?"

"Yes. Want to come and look at it with me tomorrow lunchtime?" She gave Calladine a sideways look. "I've passed by loads of times and I really like the look of the place, but I'd value your opinion."

Calladine nodded. "If I can make it." He wasn't about to mention that Zoe lived slap bang in the middle of that row of six stone cottages.

"Come on. Even policemen have to eat. Call it lunch."

"We're working on a new case," Calladine said. "Meals will be on the hoof for a while. I've got your number, so if I can make it, I'll ring."

Kitty seemed to accept this. She pointed to a table. "That's ours. Shall we sit down? I'll order a bottle of wine and you can tell me all about you and your work."

Calladine followed her to a table by the window that overlooked a small illuminated garden at the rear of the building. "Not much to tell," he admitted. "I'm a detective inspector based in Leesdon. I've always been in the police, never wanted to do anything else."

"Exciting work. Not your regular nine-to-five."

"You might think that, but believe me, chasing villains is no picnic."

"You don't look bad on it, and you don't look like a policeman either." Her eyes twinkled. "You're far too cuddly, not hard-looking enough."

Calladine didn't know whether to be flattered by the remark or not. Did "cuddly" refer to his expanding waistline?

"Besides the job, tell me something about you," she said. "Where do you live? Local?"

"Very local. Born and bred in Leesdon and I've lived in the same house most of my life. Nothing special, a stone terrace round one of the backstreets, just me and Sam, my dog. But the set-up suits me fine."

"And you told me there's no Mrs Policeman . . . ?"

He smiled. "There isn't. But I do have history. I was married and divorced by the time I was twenty-one. Some going, even for me."

"Where is she now?"

"My ex-wife died. That's when Zoe, my daughter, came north to find me. Up until then I didn't even know she existed."

"So many lost years," Kitty said wistfully.

"Indeed, but now Zoe has a little one of her own for me to fuss over. So I've been given a second chance."

As fast as tables became vacant, they filled again. Business had to be good. He was engrossed in conversation with Kitty when the sound of cutlery hitting the wooden floor got his attention. He turned to look. A young couple had knocked into a table while trying to creep out. Kitty was on her feet in an instant.

"It's okay, they've paid the bill," a waiter murmured to her.

"Then why sneak out like that?" she asked.

"Because they're two of mine." Calladine grinned at the pair and beckoned them over. "Meet DC Rockliffe and DC Bolshaw — Rocco and Alice."

"Sorry, sir, we were hoping you wouldn't see us," Alice said, blushing.

They were both dressed up, and Alice looked stunning. Instead of the prim pleated skirt and plain white shirts that made up her work uniform, she was wearing a tight, low-cut dress. She had make-up on, too. She'd made a real effort and looked quite different. It could only be for Rocco's benefit. "Are you two, er . . . ?"

"We were hoping to keep it to ourselves," Rocco admitted. "I know it's frowned upon."

"You're the same rank, and anyway it doesn't bother me, Rocco, so don't stress."

"You don't mind, sir?" He looked surprised.

"None of my business."

"It's just . . . we know what happened to DCI Greco."

Calladine shook his head slightly. Stephen Greco's dalliance with Grace had been a very different story. "He was a DI at the time and Grace a DC. When it came out that she was pregnant and he was the child's father, it sealed his fate at Oldston. You two don't even come close." He smiled.

They looked relieved. "We're hoping our private life doesn't become the latest gossip around the station," Alice said, a question in her eyes.

Kitty Lake was watching all this with an amused look on her face. "Tom," she said, taking his hand. "Leave the youngsters alone."

"It's all right," he said. "I can be discreet."

CHAPTER 7

Day Two

The following day, Calladine and Ruth met at the Duggan Centre, where Natasha was doing the PM on the murdered woman.

"Guess what I discovered last night," he said as they went in.

"You went out with that new woman, so who knows? Could have been anything."

He noted the edge to her voice. "You don't approve?"

"Not my call, but you do know that the smack she gave your car was deliberate?"

Now that did surprise him. "Kitty's not like that."

"I was watching from the sixth-floor deck of Heron House and I saw the lot. Believe me, she was parked up, just waiting for her opportunity. The woman made a beeline for your car the moment you set off. I'm not blind. I know what I saw."

"Some women can't resist me," he joked. "It was just her way of getting my attention, that's all."

"In your dreams," Ruth scoffed. "She'll have an ulterior motive, and whatever it is, you won't like it."

Calladine said nothing. His instincts said there was nothing to worry about and he liked Kitty. But Ruth was rarely wrong. She'd seen what happened and had no reason to lie to him. He decided to exercise caution with Kitty until he knew more about her. He banked the incident along with the teddy bear gift. "I'm seeing her again. She wants me to view a house with her at lunchtime."

"We're not likely to get any lunch. We've got a new case and it looks like a nasty one to me."

"I enjoyed last night," he said sulkily. "I don't meet many women these days, and Kitty is a looker. I was hoping . . ."

She punched his arm. "Grow up! You're behaving like a love-struck teen."

"She's very attractive. She runs that new restaurant, Mother's Kitchen, in Lowermill."

"Is that what you discovered?" she asked.

"No, my gossip is much juicier than that. Rocco and Alice are seeing each other."

"You sure? I'm surprised. Rocco's quite a catch but Alice, well, she's a bit of an acquired taste."

"She looked bloody gorgeous last night, Ruth, take my word for it. There was no trace of 'work Alice', and Rocco looked smitten to me."

"They've given nothing away."

"Thought they'd get into trouble. I told them that's not the case, but they still want to keep it quiet."

"But you've told me." She giggled.

"You don't count."

* * *

The two detectives were on the viewing platform, looking down at the body lying on the slab. Natasha, who had already started the PM, looked up at them. "Whoever did this spared her nothing. She was beaten hard about the body, incurring several broken bones. But it was a heavy blow to the head that killed her. There is what looks like rust embedded in her scalp, and the skull is fractured in two places. I'd say the weapon was possibly a wrench or hammer of some sort."

"A frenzied attack. What does that tell us?" Ruth whispered to Calladine.

"Someone lost it, went wild. A killer with a temper or a score to settle. I've got Rocco and Alice doing the rounds, trying to find out who she was. So far, no one's reported anyone looking like her missing."

"If she was living rough in that flat, she might not even be from round here."

"She wasn't a healthy woman," Natasha said. "Her liver is scarred — booze, I suspect. The body smelled of whisky when I first attended, and she has an enlarged heart. And then there are these." Natasha pointed to track marks on her arms and legs. "A regular user with a long-term habit, I'd say."

"How old d'you reckon she is?" Ruth asked.

"She's had a hard life and the maggots have been at her face, but at a rough guess, late fifties?"

Calladine felt his mobile vibrate. It was a text from Rocco. He had a name for the victim. After he'd asked at all the flats on the sixth floor, he found an elderly man on the floor below who said he knew her. Calladine nudged Ruth. "Her name is Rebecca or Becca O'Brien. They found a neighbour who knows her. I think we should have a chat."

At that moment, Julian entered the morgue. He looked up at the pair and nodded. "I've looked at the writing left on the wall of the flat and checked that it is the victim's blood. The word is simple enough to decipher but the image was more difficult. However, with careful cleaning we've managed. Hang on." Julian went up and showed them a photo of it on his mobile. "The word *sorry*, plus a heart shape with the initials *MR* in the centre. I'll text it to you, might prove useful."

Calladine shook his head. "Sorry, for what? Killing her? On top of all that carnage, the killer takes the time to do that.

It's unbelievable. They beat that woman half to death, finish her off with a blow to the head and then draw a little picture. What does it tell us? What does 'MR' mean if her name is Becca or Rebecca? What sort of person are we dealing with here?"

Ruth said nothing. She had an odd look on her face. "That image, the word. It rings a bell, and particularly as we now have a name."

Calladine looked at her. "Want to share?"

"Give me some time to sort the facts spinning around in my head and to check something. I'll see you back at the station," she said and turned to go.

"Hey, what about me? I'll have to walk back," he said.

"No need. There's a uniform with a car outside. I'll tell him to wait for you."

34

CHAPTER 8

Now in his sixties, Maurice Fleet had lived on the Hobfield for most of his adult life. The experience had evidently made him afraid of his own shadow. After satisfying himself that the callers really were the police, it took him several minutes to unfasten all the locks and bolts on his door.

Calladine introduced himself and the uniformed officer with him, and showed the man his warrant card.

Maurice Fleet squinted at it. "Can't be too careful. The kids round here try all sorts. They've tried to break in umpteen times, little buggers. Without the locks and the reinforcement, they'd have every stick of furniture I own. Something needs doing," he said. "I told that young detective who were 'ere but I don't think he believed me."

Calladine doubted that. Rocco didn't need telling about the dangers of the Hobfield, he'd experienced them first-hand. He got straight to the point. "You knew her? The woman one floor up from you?" Calladine asked.

Maurice folded his arms and shook his head, looking nervous. "She wasn't a friend or owt like that. I saw her around and recognized her from the past. She used to live in that same flat years ago with that daughter of hers. She were

35

another right hard nut too. By the time she were fifteen, she were out of control. Rarely went to school and no sign of a father." He grimaced. "Entire O'Brien family was a waste of space. I'm not surprised Becca ended up like that."

"Becca O'Brien. Are you sure that's her name?" Calladine asked.

"Yes, it's her all right."

"D'you know if there are any other members of the family still in Leesdon?"

"Shouldn't think so. Becca's daughter had some sort of accident. After that she wasn't quite right in th'ead. Use to talk to herself and have blackouts. She ended up in a home, I think. As far as I know there was only ever the one child and no other relatives."

"Did you hear anything the day she was killed?" Calladine asked.

"A lot of noise — enough shouting and screaming to wake the dead. I would have gone round to check on her, but I value my life too much. Whoever she was entertaining was roaring drunk and angry."

"Male or female?" Calladine asked.

"Definitely male, and local from his accent. From what little I caught, they were fighting about money. It lasted half an hour or so and then it went quiet again. I was relieved. I didn't fancy spending the night listening to that."

"Weren't you concerned when you didn't see Becca again after that?" Calladine asked.

"No. I never saw much of her anyway. The woman attracted trouble. When it went quiet, I was just glad of the peace. This flat is directly below hers, and she was always making a noise. I kept asking her to tone it down, but it made no difference. The music, the rows, it never stopped. Half the estate met up in there regularly."

"D'you know who this man is?"

"Her dealer? Pimp? Who knows? He came often enough, so there was definitely something going on," Maurice said.

36

Calladine recalled that the dead woman had been a user.

"That flat was nothing more than a drug den," Maurice continued. "Most of her visitors were youngsters, with the same half-starved look she had. They came and went, day and night."

Calladine persisted. "And you have no idea who this man might be? A name? Description? Anything you can give us will help."

Just the idea of it seemed to turn Maurice grey, and he shook his head. "I value my life, Mr Calladine. Even if the brute didn't kill me, he'd do me serious harm."

"You know the man is dangerous, so why not help us get him off the streets?" Calladine said.

"You take him in, he gets charged, goes to court, what'll he get? Some sentence that'll see him back on the estate in no time. Then he'll come looking."

"Not if we get him for murder," Calladine said.

Maurice appeared to consider this. "Try the Pheasant," he said, referring to the pub at the edge of the estate. "You're looking for a big bullish man with red hair." He glanced around as if that very man had got in somehow. "That's all I'm saying."

Calladine smiled. "Thanks. You've been very helpful."

"Want to take a look?" the PC asked once they were outside. "It's lunchtime, we could get something to eat."

"In the Pheasant? You're joking. I wouldn't eat in there for a gold clock."

"Well, just a chat with this bloke then."

Calladine considered this. "Okay, but no heroics. Someone makes a comment, ignore it. We don't want a fight, just a few answers."

CHAPTER 9

It was that heart-shaped image with the initials that had sent Ruth scurrying back to the nick. The word "sorry" had bothered her when she'd first seen it in the flat, but now, coupled with the image and finding out the victim's name, she knew why. It sparked something in her mind, a memory of an incident from years ago and a report she'd read recently.

She'd just removed her jacket and sat down when DCI Greco entered the incident room. "How is the case going?" he asked, looking at the empty whiteboard.

"I've just heard from Calladine. He's got an ID on the victim, and is on the trail of a man she argued with shortly before her death." She looked up from her computer screen and smiled at him. "Research," she said. "The word 'sorry' plus the image of a heart was written in blood on a wall in the flat the victim was found in. It reminded me of a case I looked at recently."

"Interesting," he said, looking over her shoulder.

"It was a murder, an old one. Here it is," Ruth said, pointing to the screen. "The remains were found a couple of years ago. You'd have been at Oldston and probably didn't hear of the case."

"How come you're so interested now?" he asked.

"I knew the victim," Ruth said. "If the investigating team were correct in their findings, she was a girl in my class at school." Ruth pointed to the report on the screen. "Gorse House was a rambling old place up on the hillside. Millie Reed, my friend, lived there with her granny, who owned it. She had no one else. Roughly twenty-five years ago, Millie's granny had a stroke and died. Millie disappeared. Missing Persons launched an investigation and found she'd gone to stay with a relative. She never returned and dropped off the radar. Gorse House stayed empty for years. It fell into disrepair and was eventually deemed unfit for habitation and dangerous, so it had to be torn down. During the demolition two years ago, human bones were discovered, someone spotted them amid the rubble. Forensics stated that the body had been hidden in a cavity in the cellar, possibly an old priest hole, and sealed over with wooden panels."

"Do we know anything about the bones?"

"They were those of a young female. There was a large crack in her skull, so it was presumed she'd suffered a blow to the head with something heavy, or else she fell, and that's what killed her. There was no way of knowing for sure. There were remnants of clothing found too, the skirt and blazer were polyester, thought to be part of a school uniform, Leesdon Academy, or Leesdon High as it would be then. There was a bloodstain on what was left of the skirt but with nothing to compare it with, not much use. The body was identified from a watch still hanging around the bones of the wrist. It had the name 'Millie' engraved on the back. DI Long and his team were assigned the case. He investigated but soon reached a dead end. Millie Reed hadn't been seen in years, her granny was long dead and had been cremated, so there was no DNA to match against the blood or bones. Given the age of them — the uniform, the watch, and the fact that Millie had disappeared — it was presumed the tale about her living with a relative had been wrong and the remains were hers."

"So what are you saying? That the grandmother killed her and hid the body?" Greco asked.

"There's no way of knowing exactly what happened, sir. All we know for sure is that Millie suddenly stopped attending school twenty-five years ago, shortly before her granny had the stroke, and no one's seen her since."

"Didn't anyone look into it at the time? She was a young girl, surely people were curious about what had happened to her."

"Millie would have been sixteen, a couple of years older than me. The grandmother was practically a recluse, and they were both thought to be odd, living up there on their own. Plus, it was a long time ago."

"Even so," Greco said.

"Who knows? It is easy to assume that the bones are hers, but we have no concrete proof of it. Without her granny to look out for her, Millie would have been vulnerable. She was bullied at school, and the girls who tormented her wouldn't have stopped. The fact that she was on her own would have made her seem like an easy target. So it is possible that she simply took off."

"If that's right, then it begs the question of who the bones belong to. Any ideas?"

"No, sir."

"What was she like, this Millie?" Greco asked.

"She was small and delicately built, pretty with blonde hair. Those girls from the Hobfield picked on her, bullied her mercilessly. She had a prominent mole on one of her cheeks and came in for a lot of name-calling because of it. She had no parents or other relatives, which is why she lived with her granny. No one ever got close enough to find out much about her parents. I did a check through the records and discovered that both were dead, killed in a car accident when Millie was three."

"It strikes me that that old house must have been a dangerous place to live in," he said wryly. "What's happened to arouse your interest in the case now?"

"When the place where the remains were found was examined, the word 'sorry' was written in white paint on the inside of the wooden board used to cover up the hole Millie was found in. There was also a drawing of what looked like a heart shape with the initials 'MR' in the centre. I saw the same thing drawn in blood on the wall in that flat, but the important bit is that the press got wind of the word 'sorry' at the time but not the drawing. That bit of information was never released. The initials are the same — MR, Millie Reed."

"That is odd. You say you saw the same image in the flat?"

"Yes, drawn alongside the word, just like that other one."

"Unlikely to be a coincidence then," Greco said.

"Exactly what I think. Something links the deaths — I know it does. And whatever that is could be the reason why Becca O'Brien got murdered. I'm sure one of the girls who tormented Millie was called Jade O'Brien, perhaps it was Becca's daughter."

"It's been a long time, Ruth. If you're right, then where have they been all this time and why return now?"

"They may have been here all the time, Becca on the Hobfield and Jade somewhere close by. Although I have to say I don't recall seeing her around. No one knows what really happened back then or why. Three girls from the Hobfield and Millie Reed — in all these years no one has ever spoken about it, and I have no idea where those girls are now."

"It might be an idea to find out," Greco suggested.

"DI Long did his best two years ago but he had nothing to go on and his enquiries came up blank."

"Speak to Calladine," Greco said. "See what he has to say after he's found the man O'Brien argued with. Hopefully, there's a far simpler explanation for this killing than some connection to a cold case."

"We'll see, sir, but don't bet on it. Old hatreds abound in this part of the world. Cross someone, make enemies, and the repercussions reverberate down the years."

As soon as Greco left the incident room, Ruth called Calladine on her mobile. "You should get back. We need to talk. I think we could have a problem."

CHAPTER 10

The Pheasant was empty apart from two men propping up the bar and chatting to the landlord. As soon as they spotted Calladine they fell silent. They knew who he was, most people on this estate did.

"I'm looking for a smallish bloke, skinny with red hair," Calladine said, showing them his warrant card.

The landlord shrugged. "No one who looks like that comes in 'ere. You're out o' luck, mate, got the wrong pub."

It was the same every time, and Calladine was sick of it. "No," he said. "Right pub, wrong answer." He slammed his fist down on the bar. "I will find the man with or without your help, even if I have to leave a couple of uniformed officers in here to keep an eye out for him."

The barman looked at the two customers and shook his head. "Look, mate, I don't want any trouble. All sorts come in 'ere. What's this red-haired bloke done anyway?"

"None of your business, but hold information back and I'll do you for obstruction."

"Johnno Higgs, that's who you want," one of the two customers said. "He dosses down in Heron House sometimes with that bird of his."

"Becca O'Brien?"

"Becca, yeah, that's her."

"See, that wasn't hard, was it?" Calladine scowled at the lot of them, beckoned to the PC and left. "Right. Back to the station."

"Is that your phone ringing, sir?"

Calladine reached in his pocket to take the call from Ruth.

* * *

"I have a name." Calladine came breezing in to the incident room. "Johnno Higgs. According to the old man I spoke to he was arguing with the victim shortly before her death, and word is that he provided her with drugs. Find him," he fired off at Rocco. Ruth was still busy at her desk. "What's this problem you rang about?" he asked.

"A case from the past, one of DI Long's."

"Is it relevant to the O'Brien case?"

"I think it might be," she said. "D'you recall the remains found up at Gorse House?"

Calladine nodded. "Vaguely. A young girl, thought to live there with the old woman that owned the place."

"Yes, Millie Reed, the woman's granddaughter. Her remains were thought to have been hidden in a space in the cellar of that house for years. The space was covered with wooden boards, but — and this is the interesting bit — written across them was the word 'sorry' in white paint, also a heart with the initials 'MR' in the centre. Remind you of anything?" she smiled.

Calladine sat down opposite Ruth. "Hmm. Same as with Becca. How come? Got any bright ideas?"

"Not really. I'm still trying to come up with a theory, but it's not easy. We don't even know who those bones really belonged to."

"Long reckoned it was the Reed girl they found, and that the granny must have killed her," he said. "But he had no reason to think that. There was just nothing to work with. Personally, I had my doubts."

43

"Me too," Ruth said. "I think the Gorse House killing and that of Becca O'Brien are linked, possibly the same person is responsible for both. And if they are, that means it can't have been the granny. She's been dead for years."

"What d'you base that theory on?" he said.

"The drawing of the heart shape left at both scenes and I've looked at the file. Agnes Reed had cared for Millie since she was an infant. She loved that girl, and I know she tried to protect her. I went to school with Millie Reed. She was always well turned out and clever, too. Any problems Millie had weren't caused by her gran, more likely it was the girls at school. I saw what a crap time she had. She was bullied, and the ringleader, the girl who tormented her the most, was Jade O'Brien, our dead woman's daughter." She slapped down a file on the table in front of him. "I dug this out of the archives. It makes interesting reading. Shortly before Millie disappeared, there was an incident up at Gorse House. There'd been a fight and Jade O'Brien, along with another girl, was injured, at least that's what the girls at school told the young detective who investigated."

"And that was?"

"You." Ruth smiled.

Calladine racked his brain trying to recall the case. "It was twenty-odd years ago. I hope you're not expecting me to remember much about it."

"Check your old notebooks, you might find a reference to the incident in one of them. Don't you recall anything off the top of your head?"

"Nothing that might help you now." He thought for a moment. "I do remember the house though — big, gaunt-looking thing up in the hills. Gave me the creeps."

"You were told that Jade and another girl were injured, you must have done something about that, Tom. I can't find a file on the incident or any records to suggest anyone was hurt. So we need your old notes. I want to know what your thinking was on that day."

"Look, I know exactly where my old notebooks are, filed away in the stores downstairs. They're in chronological order, but given the state of those cellars, it'll still be a job to find that particular one. If I do, I might be able to help you."

The last thing Calladine wanted to be doing was rooting around in the archives, but he knew Ruth. She wasn't going to let up. He trudged off to the station cellars to search. There, he headed for the boxes at the back of the room. Each one was labelled, and he ran his hand along them as he passed. A huge part of his working life was contained in those boxes. It gave him an odd feeling. He began to wonder how long it could continue, how many more boxes would be added, then he shook himself. This wasn't getting the job done.

He came back within the hour, carrying the relevant book in his hand. "I've written here that I put the incident down to a wind-up." He smiled. "I was a smartly dressed rookie detective still finding his feet in CID, few took me seriously back then. A girl called Sarah Hammond collared me on the road leading up to the cottage. She told me that two of her friends had been attacked by Millie Reed — that they were injured. Me and two uniforms went straight up there."

"What did you find?"

He pointed to a page in the notebook. "Nowt. It says here Agnes Reed was making the tea and the girl, Millie, wasn't even home. As we left, we saw her walking up the lane on her way back from school. She was some distance away, but it was Millie right enough. The granny hadn't the foggiest idea what I was talking about. My notes say that I reckoned that Sarah was having us on. She'd sent me off on a wild goose chase — bloody good actress to fool me like that."

"Did you speak to Millie?" Ruth asked.

"No point. The granny had told us all we needed to know, and it was obvious that Sarah had lied. Millie wasn't even there when the incident was supposed to have happened."

"What about Jade O'Brien? Speak to her?"

"Eventually, yes — in a manner of speaking. I caught up with her a couple of days later but didn't question her. She'd gone with her mother to A&E. Another overdose, it says here."

Ruth's eyes narrowed. "Why didn't you follow up with Jade? Find out if she was injured too."

Calladine flipped through his notes. "I thought she looked okay. By the time I found her at the hospital it was two days later and the middle of the night. She was half asleep by her mother's bed."

"You didn't check? Didn't even try to speak to her?"

"Apparently not." He leafed through the notes.

"What about the other girl who was allegedly injured?"

"No idea. There's no mention of her here," Calladine said. "No one ever reported anything, and there was no evidence at the house. The old woman asked me in but there was no need. Everything looked fine."

"It seems odd to me that Jade O'Brien was involved back then, and we have something similar now," Ruth said.

"You're thinking that Jade killed the grandmother?" Calladine asked.

"And possibly Millie too, all those years ago," Ruth said. "I know from school that Millie was no fighter, and her granny was no match for Jade either. What if Sarah Hammond was right, something did happen that day and later on, Jade paid the pair another visit?"

"They knew Johnno Higgs back then too," Calladine said.

"Is that relevant?"

"Yes, Ruth, a neighbour of the victim in our latest case heard two people arguing, at roughly the time of the murder. One was Becca but the other was a male. Which is why we're looking for Johnno Higgs and not a female."

"Just because the pair were heard arguing doesn't mean he killed her," Ruth said. "Do we know where Jade O'Brien is today?"

"No, but we'll have to find her. Apart from needing a word, we should tell her about her mother's death." Calladine turned toward Rocco and Alice, both of whom were listening in to the conversation. "Got that? Johnno Higgs and Jade O'Brien. See if you can find the pair of them." He thought for a second. "You could have a go at finding Sarah Hammond, too."

"Higgs has a record, sir," Alice told them. "Possession mostly. He's done time for robbery, but he's been quiet for the last couple of years."

"Anything on Jade O'Brien?" If the girl had been a bad 'un back then, chances were she was known to them too.

"No, nothing."

That surprised both Calladine and Ruth.

"Sir, I've found her," Rocco said suddenly. "Jade O'Brien is a resident at Angel Court."

Another surprise. Angel Court was a sheltered housing complex for vulnerable adults, mostly people with mental health problems "How long's she been there?"

"Twenty-four years."

CHAPTER 11

Angel Court was a collection of small bungalows and one apartment block, off the main road between the towns of Leesdon and Oldston. Set in extensive grounds, it resembled a hotel complex rather than sheltered housing.

"How much, d'you reckon?" Calladine asked as they parked up. "Stick an aged parent into care these days and it costs a fortune. Jade has been here years."

"None of her lot have money, so the state must pay, I suppose. For that to happen it must be deemed necessary for her to be here. I wonder what happened to her. Apart from being a bully, she had no problems at school. D'you know what I'm thinking, Tom?"

"Go on, surprise me."

"Perhaps Jade was hurt that day up at Gorse House and her being here today is the result."

"Another leap," he said. "You're full of them today."

"Did you actually have a conversation with Jade back then, speak to her about the incident? No, you didn't — you said so yourself," Ruth said.

"I told you, she was dozing by her mother's bed. I didn't get another chance after that."

"Did you consider that perhaps she wasn't asleep but hurt in some way?"

Calladine scratched his head. The thought had obviously never crossed his mind.

Ruth had rung ahead so they were expected. They were met in the reception area of the apartment block by Mary Kershaw, the manager. Calladine introduced them. "We'd like to speak to Jade O'Brien. Her mother has been killed and she should know, but apart from that we'd like a word with her about a matter from the past."

She gasped. "Her mother's dead? How dreadful. Becca was never up to much as a parent and the pair rarely met, but Jade does talk about her occasionally." She looked from one detective to the other. "Killed, you said. An accident?"

"No. I'm afraid Becca was murdered," Calladine said. "We're investigating and it would help to have some background, including her relationship with Jade."

The woman's expression changed. She wasn't keen on the idea. "Jade has done very well with us, given her problems, but her memory isn't good. She doesn't recall much, and I hesitate to dredge up anything that will upset her. This matter from the past — important, is it?"

Ruth looked at Calladine, who was gazing out of the window. The Jade she recalled from school had been bright, capable of going far with the right guidance. She certainly hadn't been someone who needed sheltered accommodation or had memory problems. "What happened to her? How come she ended up here?"

"You know I can't discuss a resident's medical history with you, not without a warrant or Jade's approval. All I'm prepared to say is that she's here because of an accident years ago. She had a nasty knock to the head. It resulted in an internal bleed that wasn't picked up at the time. Eventually, she lost consciousness and didn't come round for many days. When she did, she wasn't the same girl."

"Do you know how long ago this was?" Calladine asked.

"Twenty-odd years, I guess. If Jade agrees, I can dig out the file and let you look at it."

"Is it likely she will?" Ruth asked. "I mean how . . . how ill is she?"

"This isn't a hospital, Sergeant, or a prison. It's a sheltered environment for vulnerable people. They live in the apartments or bungalows here as independently as they can manage. The more able among them come and go as they please. If they need help, they get it. We give them a full social calendar and encourage them to keep in touch with family and friends. While she's in our care, Jade thrives. However, she doesn't do well on the outside. She can't cope with noise for a start."

"Does Jade ever leave the complex on her own?" Calladine asked.

"Sometimes, when she's having a good day. The library is a favourite of hers. Someone from here drops her off and picks her up at an agreed time."

Definitely not the Jade Ruth remembered. The girl she knew at school wouldn't have wasted her time reading. "Can we speak to her?" Ruth asked.

"I'll take you to her apartment."

* * *

Jade O'Brien's apartment was on the ground floor of the three-storey block. Mary Kershaw rang the bell and the three of them waited. Ruth had no idea what to expect. The Jade she remembered was a vicious bully, a girl more suited to prison than the peaceful seclusion of an Angel Court.

A woman opened the door and stared at them for several seconds. Apart from the effects of the passing years, she looked much as Ruth remembered her — still stick thin and with the same unruly dark hair, now greying.

"You're police," Jade said finally. "I can always tell. And you," she pointed at Ruth, "you're that interfering bitch from school. I didn't like you then, so what're doing bothering me now?"

50

"You remember me?" Ruth was surprised. At least if Jade did recall her, it would save a lot of explaining.

"No . . . I'm not sure. I might if I think hard enough. Perhaps you just remind me of someone," Jade said.

"My name's Ruth, and you're right, we used to know each other at school. Can we come in and chat for a bit?"

"Just you and Mary but not the bloke." She pointed at Calladine. "He looks shifty. I don't trust him."

Ruth gave him a wry smile. "You heard the lady, you're shifty and banned to the corridor."

Ruth and Mary Kershaw followed Jade inside and she locked the door behind them. "Don't want that bloke chancing his arm."

"He's no danger," Ruth assured her.

"They're all dangerous, don't be taken in. Men are all the same. My mother used to tell me that."

"As a matter of fact, your mother is the reason we've come to see you," Ruth said.

"Why? What's she done now?"

Ruth watched as Jade lit a cigarette and moved to the open window. She seemed nervous.

"I haven't seen her in months, and she doesn't ring anymore either."

"I'm afraid she's dead," Ruth said as gently as she could.

There was a few moments' silence. Then, to Ruth's surprise, Jade started to laugh. "Stupid woman. She overdosed, didn't she?"

Her reaction was unexpected, but it meant Jade knew about her mother's habit. It was something. "She was murdered, Jade."

She shrugged. "Didn't pay up then. Dealers don't like that, particularly those who supply Johnno."

"You remember Johnno?" Ruth asked.

"His name is stuck in my head for some reason. I might recognize him if I saw him, but then again, I might not."

"We think your mother's death has something to do with what happened to you, the accident you had a long time ago," Ruth said.

"What accident?" Jade flashed a look at Mary. "I'm okay, aren't I? I'm not hurt. What's she on about?"

"The accident, the attack you suffered before you came here," Mary said. "Remember, Jade? You've told me about it many times. The fight you and your friends had up at Gorse House with that girl, Millie. She hurt you, hit your head with a hammer, you said."

Jade stood staring into space, her face suddenly blank and her eyes glazed. Mary darted forward and took the cigarette from her. "You're okay, Jade. Sit down. Let it pass."

"What's up with her?" Ruth whispered.

"She'll be all right in a moment or two. It's a form of epilepsy."

"The result of the bang on the head?" Ruth asked. She looked at Jade's face. Despite the seizure, she knew there had been an argument up at Gorse House that day. It was even possible that when Calladine had caught up with Jade at the hospital, she wasn't asleep but semi-conscious and the idiot hadn't noticed. "Does this happen often?"

"Yes, Sergeant. Her memory is very patchy and she is subject to seizures when she gets stressed. She also has severe mood swings. As well as everything else."

"I'm sorry. She's certainly very different from the girl I knew at school. I see that she's spoken to you about Gorse House. Has she told you what happened?" Ruth asked.

"A little. There was a fight, I believe, and Jade was hit on the head. Sometimes Jade remembers and sometimes not. Some things from the past have stuck — names and the like — but generally her memories go back only weeks. After that they fade and disappear or become confused," Mary said. "She has nightmares, and when she wakes, she sometimes talks of a girl who hit her, but she's never said very much."

"Well, there's no doubt she suffered a head injury," Ruth said. "I'd like to know who hit her. It might have been a girl called Millie, but it could just as easily have been that same girl's granny."

"Whatever happened, it's a pity the injury wasn't spotted sooner. If Jade had received proper care, the outcome for her might have been very different."

"I knew Jade at school, her friends too," Ruth said. "They were a hard bunch, girls you didn't cross. Millie was quiet, not at all violent. Jade bullied her. It is possible that she and her mates went up to Gorse House that day and things got out of hand. Jade was injured, but Millie came off worst in the end. We believe it is her remains that were found up there two years ago."

Jade suddenly came to life. "That's a lie," she yelled. "I never touched the kid. I don't know what happened to her."

"Why are you asking about this now?" Mary Kershaw asked.

"I believe there's a link between the death at Gorse House and that of Jade's mother all these years later," Ruth said. "When was the last time Jade was out alone?"

"I'll have to check the calendar, but I know she went out on Monday, to Leesdon library as usual."

That would fit. "What time did she return?"

"Actually, it was about eight thirty. I remember because she came back on the bus, which surprised me. Usually she'd ring one of the carers and get picked up. When Jade got in, she said she'd been reading and forgot the time."

"Can we take a look at your medical record while we're here?" Ruth asked Jade.

Jade shrugged. "Fill your boots, but don't expect to find much. I'm a headcase, have been since the attack."

CHAPTER 12

Ruth and Calladine followed Mary Kershaw back to her office. "I'm really not happy about this," Mary said.

"Jade doesn't seem to mind," Ruth replied.

"She doesn't understand."

"Why? She's of sound mind, isn't she?" Ruth asked.

Mary made a dismissive gesture. "Yes, but that's not what I mean. She has no idea what's in those records. Suppose you see something that incriminates her?"

"I don't see a list of medication and write-ups of doctor's appointments being that damning," Calladine said dryly. He tapped Ruth's arm. "Did she say anything?"

"She reckons she was in the library at the time her mother was killed," Ruth said. "It needs checking out, and as I thought, she was injured up at Gorse House."

They went into the office and sat down. "The attack left her with memory loss and prone to bouts of severe depression and epilepsy," Mary said over her shoulder while she searched out the file. "Initially when she left hospital, she was in her mother's care but that didn't work at all. As you know, Becca was an addict. She left stuff lying around the flat, and within a week, Jade had overdosed. She mistook what her mother was

54

taking for her own medication. Jade was hospitalized again and almost didn't make it. That's when she was put into our care, and she has been here ever since. When she takes her medication regularly, Jade is fine. She takes care of herself and doesn't get into arguments with the other residents. But if she lets her regime slip, all hell lets loose."

"What does that mean?" Ruth asked.

Mary gave a heavy sigh. "She gets into fights. Some of them have been nasty. She broke another resident's arm last year. Jade fell into a blinding rage and went for her. If one of the carers hadn't been on hand, Jade might have killed the woman."

"Violent and unpredictable, you've got your hands full," Calladine said. "How does Jade act when these outbursts are over?"

"Well, sorry of course," Mary said. "In fact she wrote the woman a letter saying as much. No prompting from the staff, Jade did it all on her own. I think she was genuinely upset at losing it like that."

"Thanks. You've been very helpful," Calladine said. "Can I ask that you try to keep Jade restricted to the premises until we've completed our investigations? No more trips to Leesdon library for a while."

"I'll do my best."

* * *

"What d'you think?" Ruth asked. "Is Jade our killer?"

"She could be, but we really need to know where she was when her mother was murdered. A clearer idea of what went on up at Gorse House would help, too." Calladine frowned. "What's bothering me is the timescale. If Jade did kill the Reed girl, why wait all these years to strike again?"

"Something set it off. Someone's said or done something. Jade is unpredictable, so who knows?" Ruth said.

"And why kill her mother? Becca O'Brien wasn't even involved in the original case."

"We don't know that," Ruth said. "She might have taken it on herself to go up there and give the Reeds a piece of her mind. Anyway, according to you, there wasn't even a case. You went up there and found nothing. The girls you spoke to had nowt to say. We might find something to link her to Becca's murder but we're woefully short of evidence for her killing Millie."

"Someone killed the poor girl, and I tend to go with your theory that it wasn't the granny. We're unlikely to get much forensically from anything that was found back then, so let's hope Julian finds something helpful at Becca's flat."

"What about the bones?" Ruth said. "Julian could get DNA from them."

"He could but we've nothing to match it to, and then there's the budget," Calladine said.

"But should we find something?"

"Then we'll think again."

"Want to visit the library on the way back?" Ruth asked.

"CCTV. What d'you think?" he said.

"I've never noticed, but they might have. They might remember her, too."

"We should find Johnno Higgs, bring him in," Calladine said.

His mobile rang. An unknown number and a woman he didn't recognize.

"My name is Debra Weller. I'm from the firm of solicitors currently working for Marilyn Fallon. Can we meet up? There's something I'd like to discuss with you."

Marilyn was his cousin Ray's wife and was doing time for murdering him. Calladine was curious — what did she need a solicitor for? "Is there a problem?"

"No, but I'd appreciate a chat."

"When did you have in mind?" he said.

"This evening if possible, I'm staying at the Leesdon Arms Hotel for a few days. Meet me in the reception area at 7 p.m."

Calladine finished the call and turned to Ruth. "That was a weird one. Some solicitor wants to meet me, to talk about Marilyn."

"What's to talk about? The woman's locked up for killing Ray." She smiled. "As much as that might please you, it's against the law."

"Well, a quick chat can't do any harm. I'm meeting her tonight."

Ruth's grin broadened. "Her, eh? Two new women in one week. A record even for you, Calladine."

CHAPTER 13

Leesdon library didn't have CCTV but they did know Jade O'Brien. The woman on the counter pulled a face at the mention of her name.

"There's always a performance when she comes in. She upsets people, sits talking to herself when she's reading. She makes frequent phone calls disturbing everyone else. No matter how many times I tell her, nothing changes."

"When did you last see her?" Ruth asked.

"Monday afternoon. I remember because she argued with Bert Thompson, a regular of ours. She had a right go at him over there," she nodded at a table. "I had to intervene because of the noise. Jade didn't like that, had a strop at me then left."

"D'you recall what time that was?" Ruth asked.

"Yes, about 4 p.m. The kids were starting to come in after school."

"Thank you, that's been a great help," Ruth said.

"You know what that means," she said once they were outside. "If she left here at four and didn't get back to Angel Court until eight thirty, that's four and a half hours unaccounted for."

"It gives her opportunity," Calladine agreed. "But the neighbour heard Becca arguing with a man."

"So, perhaps Jade was there too, and the man shouted at both of them. We can't rule her out, Tom."

"But what's her motive? Why would she kill her own mother?"

"Jade isn't right, is she?" Ruth said. "She has mental health issues."

"Okay, she's a suspect, but we'll keep an open mind."

When they returned to the station, Alice was busy working at her computer. Rocco was out.

"He's gone after Johnno Higgs," Alice said.

"Good, we need a word with him."

Ruth phoned Julian from her desk. "Would you do something for me?" she asked. "The Reed case — some bones found two years back up at the ruins of Gorse House. A large panel of wood covered the hole where the remains were found. There was writing on one side of it. Would you compare it with the writing you found in Becca O'Brien's flat?"

"You've got a theory?"

"Yes, Julian. I've got a nasty feeling the same person killed both Millie and Becca."

"The writing on the board was done in paint, untidily as I recall — just like the writing in the flat. Given we now have the heart-shaped image at both scenes, you could be right. The Reed girl was killed some twenty-odd years ago. Have you considered why there's such a gap of time between them?"

"That's still a work in progress. I'll wait and see what you come up with first." Ruth finished her call.

"Uniform have been on the Hobfield all morning looking for Higgs with Rocco," Alice said. "A PC's just rung in to say they've found him in the Pheasant, and he's been drinking heavily."

"Just what we need. A drunk dealer."

* * *

Calladine was in his office going through Long's file on the Reed case. He could barely recall the investigation, but the file, together with his notes from the time, helped bring the memories back. Sarah Hammond who'd told him about the incident hadn't really said much at all. He had tried to press her but didn't get far. He'd been a young, inexperienced detective back then. He knew better now. Sarah and her group were all from the Hobfield and trained from birth not to talk to the police. Sarah did admit to knowing Millie and said her friends liked her. Calladine had asked about her report of the alleged fight at Gorse House and the injuries sustained by two of the girls, one of them Jade, but he'd drawn a blank. Sarah said she'd been mistaken, and they hadn't been up there but had met Jade running away from the place. Given Jade's injuries she'd presumed that something had happened at Millie's. She's apologized and said she'd lied for a dare. The file noted that Sarah Hammond was nervous, a girl with a slight stammer who had flushed at the very mention of the house. Calladine noted that he had intended to speak to her again, find out the truth of the matter but other work came up and he never did. Twenty-five years later, he would dearly like to have another go. That girl had been afraid of something, and he knew that the Calladine of today could persuade her to talk.

"Sarah Hammond," he called to Alice. "How's that going?"

"Not well. There is no marriage certificate, no death recorded either, so I presume she's alive somewhere. I'm still looking, got a few more things to try."

"She used to live on the Hobfield, so she might still be local. I need a chat with her about the Reed case," he said. "It's important. She could be the only person left who knows what really happened up there that day."

CHAPTER 14

Two uniformed officers brought Johnno Higgs into the station. He was put in an interview room and given a mug of strong coffee to sober him up.

Calladine and Ruth watched him for a while through the two-way window. Ruth shook her head. "You'll be lucky to get any sense out of him. Bet he doesn't know what day it is, never mind what he was doing several nights ago."

"We can but try." Calladine sighed. "Right now, he's the best we've got."

"We'd better give him a while, a bucket too from the look of him. The cleaners won't be happy if he throws up all over the floor."

Ruth was right. Calladine nodded to the uniform who was watching with them. "We'll let Higgs stew for an hour or so before we speak to him."

He was about to return to his own office when Greco called to him from the corridor. "Tom, a word. Come in and close the door."

What did he want? Calladine was tempted to pretend he hadn't heard him but changed his mind. It might be something to do with Lazarov.

It was. Greco passed him a printout of an email he'd received that afternoon from Huddersfield CID. They had information that Lazarov was now living in Manchester. No address, just confirmation that he'd been seen several times in and around the Fallowfield area of the city.

"Our colleagues at Manchester Central will pass on any information they get. But as Huddersfield say, he has to have moved for a reason. Let's hope it doesn't involve you," Greco said.

"He's back to settle old scores, it's that simple. Lazarov doesn't usually operate on our side of the Pennines. Something's brought him here, and that makes me doubly nervous."

"Your family is safe. We've put measures in place, and you've warned your daughter."

Calladine nodded, but realistically what use was one female FLO against the likes of Lazarov?

"If I get anything else, you'll be the first to know," Greco said. "How's the new case doing? Got anything to work with yet?"

"We're interviewing people who knew the victim. Got one in the cells as we speak, we're just giving him time to sober up."

"Good, the sooner we nail this one the better. That estate is bad enough without an unsolved murder stirring things up."

Calladine said nothing. The man had only been here two minutes, he couldn't possibly know what made the Hobfield tick, or much about the people who lived there. Calladine could count on the fingers of one hand the number of times Greco had visited the place. Becca O'Brien was a virtual recluse and an addict. Sad as it was, it was unlikely she would be missed, and few would mourn her passing. As for the Hobfield, the folk who lived there would carry on as they always had, turning a blind eye and saying nothing. Understanding the way the estate worked took a lifetime of being among the folk who lived there.

Calladine stuffed the piece of paper in his pocket and made his way back to the incident room.

"Ruth's gone to get a sandwich before the interview," Alice said.

"Hope she gets one for me. Missed my lunch."

* * *

Ruth had just paid for a couple of sandwich packs when she spotted Greco looking at the menu board. "Not much choice," she said. "You might be better leaving it until later."

"Can't, I'm actually leaving early. Thought I'd grab something to eat on the way. I've a feeling tea might be late tonight."

"Going anywhere nice?" she asked.

"First I'm off for a chat with Superintendent Quaid and Ronan Sinclair, the curator at the museum in Lowermill."

"Trouble?"

"I hope not, in view of what's happening. We're getting the Leesworth Hoard back for a month or so."

"About time," Ruth said. "Most folk around here have never seen it. It was found not two miles away, buried up on the hills. The British Museum took the lot and that was that. Want to have a look and it means a trip to London."

"Well they'll get the chance soon," he said.

"Mind you, someone will have to lay on security," Ruth said. "All that Celtic gold and jewellery, very tempting."

"That's why we're having the meeting. Sinclair is jittery and Quaid is keen to put his mind at rest," Greco said.

"Fair enough, but I hope the super doesn't think we've got time to babysit it."

"No, but he has asked if someone from the local police will appraise the building, point out the weak spots, you know the sort of thing," Greco said. "A private security company will look after it while it's here. Can't be too careful though, the Hoard is worth an absolute fortune. After that, the little one's got his six-month check-up. Grace will take him, so I'm charged with looking after the two girls."

Ruth nodded. "I know what that's like. You do right to make the time. You can get so wrapped up in the job that everything else takes a back seat." She gave him a puzzled look. "Six months, you said. I thought he was older than that. He's getting on for a year by now, surely."

"No, Ruth, you're making the assumption everyone else does," Greco said wearily. "You'll have heard the gossip and know that Grace got pregnant in Brighton. We were set to make a go of it then, but she lost that baby. The poor soul didn't make it to the first scan, no heartbeat."

Ruth was shocked, she'd had no idea, and she doubted anyone else had either. "I'm sorry, Stephen. That must have been hard on you both."

"To be brutally honest, Ruth, I felt nothing but relief at the time. It was my way out. Me and Grace talked it through and decided a clean break was best."

"That didn't happen though. You got married."

"A week or so after we split, I realized I'd made a mistake, and that I was truly fond of Grace and didn't want to lose her. We agreed to try again, were married within the month and shortly after that she was pregnant again. Little Stephen is the outcome."

"Ended well then," Ruth said. "But like you say, people are still gossiping about you and Grace." Greco shrugged. "Like me, they have no idea what really happened. The tale of you, Grace and Brighton followed you from Oldston. People make assumptions and I'm afraid gossip and rumour follows." Ruth paused, wondering how Greco was taking this. She couldn't tell from the look on his face. "Can I make a suggestion? Don't take this the wrong way, but you shouldn't bottle things up. Let people in. You'll be surprised what a help this lot can be when things get rough. Look at me and Tom." She grinned. "I've got some past, believe me. Look at the huge mistake I made over Rob Harris — the man was a serial killer for heaven's sake. But I didn't hide it, or why. It was a reaction to Jake walking out on me, and people understood that. As for Tom, he's a disaster zone where women are concerned. I think the best way to deal with the tittle-tattle is to be upfront. That way no one has anything to whisper about."

He didn't look convinced. "I'm not given to discussing my feelings or problems outside close family."

"My advice, for what it's worth, is to try and change, Stephen. That way you'll make more friends and find people understand and want to help." Greco looked unsure. "D'you want me to put the team right about you and Grace? It would put a stop to the whispers."

"If you can do that without making an issue of it, I'd be grateful, Ruth." He smiled at her.

CHAPTER 15

Johnno Higgs had a record. Calladine looked at the file in front of him and saw that he was forty-five years old. A few years older than Jade, but a good dozen years younger than Becca.

"You've been a friend of Becca O'Brien's and her daughter for years now," Calladine began. "You must be upset about Becca's death."

Johnno Higgs took a long slug from the water on the table and swallowed hard. He looked grey and tired after his hard night's drinking. "I heard about what happened. I know her because we live in the same block."

"I think your relationship with that pair goes further back than that, Johnno," Calladine said.

"Tell us about Jade," Ruth said.

"What about her?" Higgs shrugged.

"D'you know what happened to make her the way she is?"

"Yeah, course I do. She got belted round th'ead by the girl what used to live at Gorse House. Jade were never the same after that." He tapped his head. "Not right upstairs."

"Have you seen her since that time?"

"Now and again."

"Does she ever talk about it?" Ruth asked.

"She doesn't remember much but I do." He nodded. "The day it happened, Jade and some of her pals went up there after school, invited like. It were a big mistake. That kid, Millie, lost it and clobbered two of them."

Not the tale Sarah Hammond had told him. Calladine waited while Higgs downed another glass of water. "So, two girls were attacked. What's the name of the other one?"

"It were Jade's best mate. Kaz something, I think."

"Is she still local?" Calladine asked.

"No. Becca told me she got a job on the coast somewhere, near Whitby. She never came back, don't blame her either. Her mother was every bit as bad as Becca. That day they were both off their heads and ended up in hospital. I presume the kid saw her chance and buggered off."

"D'you have a full name for her?" Calladine asked.

"No, just Kaz."

"Why didn't you come forward at the time? We could have done something about the assault," Calladine said.

"Like what?" he scoffed. "That girl Millie wasn't like the ones from the Hobfield, too well spoken and all neat and tidy like. Anyway, her granny would have twisted anything Jade said. She was a right piece of work she was."

Calladine was surprised. He'd been unable to discover much at all about Agnes Reed. "Why d'you say that, Johnno?"

"She'd not listen to a word said against the girl, always turned a blind eye. But the kid was a bad 'un, take my word for it. She went for Jade and her friend, and look how it left Jade," Higgs said.

"They shouldn't have bullied the kid like they did. They were older, bigger. Jade and her friends probably thought they could sort her no bother, and pushed her to the brink," Ruth said.

"No excuse. You're forgetting how badly Jade was hurt," Higgs said.

"D'you remember any other names?" she said.

"Not really. They were just Jade's mates. They were too young for me, so I never took much notice."

"When was the last time you saw Becca?" Ruth asked.

Higgs looked worried, talk of Becca obviously upset him. "Look, you're not pinning that one on me. I never lifted a finger against her."

Calladine decided it was time to test his theory that the loud voice heard that night belonged to Johnno Higgs. "But you were there the night she was killed. The pair of you were heard arguing."

Higgs looked away, but he didn't deny it. "Becca was easy to argue with," he said. "It was always about the same thing — she wanted more dope and I'd refuse. It was the same the night she died. The woman was off her 'ead as it was, any more was a real risk to her life." He paused, took a deep breath. "This isn't easy to say but given what happened, I know what I should've done, got her some help there and then, but I didn't. I left Becca alone and went off to the Pheasant as usual."

So it was his voice Maurice Fleet had heard. Johnno Higgs hadn't tried to deny it either.

"When you left, was she okay?" Ruth asked.

"Not okay exactly, she wanted more heroin and when I said no, she said she'd ring someone else."

"D'you know who that was?" Calladine asked.

"No. I usually provided Becca with what she needed," Higgs said.

"She must have been sure of this new dealer. Are you certain you've no idea who it is?" Calladine said.

"No, but word has it they're new and set to take over."

That was worrying. Johnno Higgs only dealt in small amounts and mostly to people he knew. For a while now Calladine had been thinking that the field was wide open for a full-scale takeover.

"Did you see anyone else on the deck that night?" he asked.

"No. Place was like the grave."

"And what time did you leave?" Calladine asked.

"It was almost nine. I know cause I just made the darts match at the pub, and that starts at nine on the dot."

"D'you know what happened to Becca's mobile? We didn't find it with the body."

"No idea. She had it the last time I saw her. Always had the thing in her hand."

"Thanks," Calladine said. "We'll probably want to talk to you again, Johnno, so don't go leaving the area."

"Have you told Jade?" Higgs asked.

"Yes, although it was difficult to judge how she took it," Calladine said.

"Like I said, the woman's not all there."

CHAPTER 16

Back in the incident room, Ruth and Calladine went over the interview. "He wasn't as difficult to deal with as I'd expected. Given he's a dealer, Johnno Higgs didn't seem to mind talking to us at all," Ruth said.

"Don't be taken in, he'll be holding back. He's been dragged in here enough times and he knows the ropes by now. He's well versed in what to leave out," Calladine said.

"I thought it went well, and he did tell us about the new dealing. We didn't know about that," she said.

"We need to get more information on that — who is taking the lead for starters. As for the murder, it depends on what Forensics turn up." Calladine rubbed his head. "Becca was murdered. Her identity is not in question, but what about the bones found at Gorse House?"

"Millie Reed," Ruth said.

"But is it really her? What actual proof do we have?"

"The fact she's not been seen in years, the watch found on the wrist bones, what else is there?" she said.

"Not much, granted. But there is that bloodstain on the skirt."

"We don't have anything to do a DNA match against, Tom. It's the same as with the bones. The house has gone, the granny's dead, so there's nothing left."

"Will you dig out the evidence Long gathered when the bones were found? See if there was anything he came up with that might help us."

She made a face. "It'll all be in storage, and you know what that means."

He did. Time spent in a dusty cellar containing too many boxes. He'd been down there to find his old notebooks. Even knowing exactly where they were, he'd still had to negotiate the metres of shelving and shuffle boxes around. "It's all we've got, Ruth. We're looking for a killer. We think there's a link between the deaths of Becca and Millie, but we don't know for sure that the Reed girl is dead."

"We could do with a word with the others who were involved that day. Have another look in the file, see if any of them are still local," Ruth suggested.

"Okay, you and Alice find whatever we've got tomorrow," he said.

"Fine, now I'm off," she said, grabbing her things. "You seeing your new lady friend tonight?"

"Which one?"

"You tell me." Ruth grinned.

"I'm meeting that solicitor in the Leesdon Arms later. She wants to talk about Marilyn, can't think why."

"What about the other one, Kitty?" she asked.

"I'll ring her and explain."

"I was talking to Greco earlier. I told him he should be a bit more like you. Stop being so secretive, let it all out for the team to pick over. That way they'll quickly lose interest and see him as just another bloke."

"I'd prefer it if you didn't pick over my love life, thank you."

"You know what I'm getting at. Look at the rumours surrounding Greco and Grace for a start. We've all misjudged the man," she said. "The kid he had with Grace is only six months old, you know what that means."

Calladine hadn't really thought about it. "What?"

"The first pregnancy failed, they split, made up and had another go at making it work. The kid they've got now was born after they married and has nothing to do with Brighton."

Calladine considered this. "So? How does that change things? He's still a weirdo."

"No he isn't, He's just another member of the team with his fair share of life's problems. We have to put the gossips right. I'll take our lot and you can tell Long. Thorpe treats the whole thing like a joke. He sniggers like a big kid every time Greco's name is mentioned, and it's not fair."

"Greco brings it on himself," Calladine said.

"No he doesn't, and besides, I like him. You might too if you only tried harder."

Calladine pulled a face. He and Greco had settled into an easy sort of amicability, but that didn't mean becoming best buddies with the man.

Ruth made for the door. "Enjoy your night and keep out of trouble."

That would depend on what Debra Weller wanted. Calladine went into his office, sat at his desk and scanned through Higgs's statement. It was as the neighbour had said, the argument, then the silence. Providing Higgs was telling the truth that meant only one thing, someone else had gone to Becca's flat later on. But unlike Johnno Higgs, they'd been as quiet as the night and hadn't been seen. Another dealer? Jade? Or someone as yet unknown?

Calladine tossed the statement into his desk drawer. He'd had enough for the day. Time to go home, walk Sam, his dog, and go for his meeting at the Leesdon Arms.

CHAPTER 17

Debra Weller was younger than Calladine had expected, probably about thirty. She was tall with cropped fair hair, slender verging on too thin, and casually dressed in jeans and a shirt.

"Glad you could make it," she said. "I've got us a table and told them we'd be eating. Hope you don't mind."

Calladine didn't. Apart from the dog, he had an empty house to go back to. "You said on the phone that this was about Marilyn," he said, taking a seat.

"I've ordered you a beer, that all right?"

Calladine nodded. A beer would suit him nicely. She was drinking wine, and he wasn't a fan.

"Marilyn's been given parole and I'd like your help."

Parole? Marilyn was doing time for murder, and it was way too soon for the powers that be to consider releasing her. "How come?" he asked. "Who wangled that one for her?"

Debra Weller gave him an unimpressed look. "I assure you, it's all above board. She's been very helpful. Marilyn has given the police information that's led to several cases her husband was involved in being cleared up."

"Happy to dob him in now he's dead. That woman wouldn't say a word against him while he lived. I should know, I questioned her often enough."

"That's because she was too scared, Mr Calladine," she explained. "Ray Fallon controlled everything in Marilyn's life — in the end even what went on inside her head."

That didn't sound like the Marilyn he remembered. She was a strong-willed woman, more than able to stand her own corner. That was what Ray had liked about her. "You've met her, I don't know how you can say that with a straight face."

"Have you heard the term 'coercive control'?"

Calladine knew very well what it meant. Debra Weller was trying to tell him that Ray bullied Marilyn into being the obedient little housewife who didn't open her mouth unless he let her. That was nonsense, not how it was at all. Marilyn could give as good as she got. He shook his head. "If ever Ray tried laying down the law with Marilyn, he lost. She gave him a black eye more than once in the early days. Marilyn was a hard woman back then. Ray wouldn't waste his time trying to get the better of her. Him and Marilyn were a team. For a while, both were as bad as each other."

"You're mistaken. That was a mere front, things weren't like that at all. Marilyn was too ashamed to speak out. The woman didn't have access to her friends, her freedom, or any money to speak of. He gave her a meagre allowance each week and she spent all of that on the dog."

"Who's told you this rubbish?"

"Marilyn. She gave a full statement along with information about Ray. The fact she killed him isn't in dispute, but after due consideration the court decided that Marilyn was trying to protect herself from her husband's cruelty. Some of the incidents she told us about have been backed up by people they both knew."

"Which people?" Calladine laughed. "I wonder how much she paid them." He swilled down the rest of his beer. He couldn't listen to any more of this. "She's spun you lot a yarn and you've fallen for it. Turn on the waterworks, did she? She's good at that. She gives you details of jobs Ray did, tells you about secret accounts where money is stashed, and you fall for it. The woman is a master, hardly surprising since she had Ray for a teacher." Calladine put down his beer glass a bit more forcefully than he'd intended. "You've been had, lady, that's all there is to it."

Debra Weller coloured up. She cleared her throat. "I'm not that easily duped, believe me. That woman suffered for years, so it's hardly surprising she did what she did. Any woman in her position would be sorely tempted to do the same."

Calladine looked Debra Weller in the eyes. "There was no love lost between me and Ray, but she killed him in cold blood, never forget that, and when he was helpless to stop her. He was dying anyway, for God's sake. The man had a heart problem. Apart from which, he was no longer a danger to Marilyn — he was behind bars."

"He was still calling the shots, telling her what to do, what to think, even from his prison cell."

Calladine shook his head. This was rubbish.

"Okay, Mr Calladine, we aren't going to agree. I accept that, but I still need your help."

He sighed. "What do you want from me?"

"Marilyn needs somewhere to stay, preferably with someone who knows her. Currently she's in a hostel and that's not good for her. Shortly I'll approach the court and ask if she can relocate to her sister's in Cumbria, but until they agree, she's asked if you would take her in. Apparently, you've been taking care of her dog."

"Sam? What's the dog got to do with anything?"

"Marilyn misses him. The animal was a large part of her life. She's looking forward to having him back."

Calladine had grown fond of Sam. The dog was good company, and he didn't want to give him up. "What if I say no?"

"Then I'll have to find somewhere else and that will take time. Finding a place to take Marilyn and her dog will be tricky."

He didn't like the sound of that either. Sam wasn't getting any younger and he had settled down well with him. The dog wouldn't appreciate being dragged around.

"How long's she been out?" he asked.

"Two weeks, and she reckons the hostel is as bad as the prison. She needs somewhere, Mr Calladine, and you're her last chance."

"I'm a policeman, she's the widow of a gangster, think what sort of position that puts me in."

"She's out on appeal," Debra Weller said firmly. "Marilyn has done nothing wrong. What happened that day with her husband was down to coercion and her being terrified. You have to help her now. You're her last chance."

What choice did he have? "Okay," he agreed finally, "but it's a temporary arrangement, understand?"

"Yes, of course. She won't be any trouble. Marilyn knows the rules. She'll hardly leave the house and not give you any cause for concern, I promise."

"You can't promise that. You don't even know the woman. The person you've just described is a fantasy, Ms Weller, not Marilyn Fallon."

* * *

Calladine didn't wait for the promised meal. He left the Leesdon Arms and marched off towards home. Debra Weller was off her head if she believed all that nonsense about Marilyn. He'd heard enough and didn't want to get into a slanging match with her.

He decided to pick something up from the chip shop on the High Street on the way home.

"Can't get away from you, can I?" Ruth called from inside.

He was pleased to see her, a welcome diversion from the confusion going on inside his head.

"What're you doing here?" he asked.

"I gave Harry his tea earlier, intending to save mine until I'd got him to bed. But then I got into a blazing row on the phone with Jake. After that, I couldn't be bothered cooking."

"What's he done now?" Calladine asked.

"He'd promised to take the little lad out tomorrow and now he reckons he can't. It'll be down to that bloody woman he's taken up with," she said.

"Not good. Harry should come first. Mind you, my evening's not been much better. I met that solicitor woman. Marilyn's out — can you believe that?"

"Nothing about the justice system surprises me anymore, Tom."

"Oh it's worse than that. She wants me to put her up. I tried to say no — I mean, how can I? She's a convicted murderer and I'm a policeman, but she played the Sam card, so I gave in. What else could I do? When she sees how happy and contented he is with me she'll think differently. I have to persuade her to leave him behind where he's happy."

She smiled. "Call yourself a policeman. You're nothing but a big softy." It was Ruth's turn to be served. "What d'you want?" she asked. "Shall I get us both a chippy tea and we'll go back to mine?"

"Yeah, that sounds great. Got any beer in?"

CHAPTER 18

Day Three

When Calladine arrived the following morning, Ruth wasn't in the incident room, but her jacket was over her chair as usual.

"She's gone for a rummage through the archive," Alice told him. "She was in here at 7 a.m. on a mission and I haven't seen her since."

She'd be looking for anything to do with Gorse House and Millie Reed. His mobile buzzed. It was a text from Julian, he wanted a word. "I'll be in my office," he told Alice.

"Tom, we've got something," Julian said. "We've been trying to make sense of the crime scene, not easy given the mess the killer left behind. There was blood all over the floor, and on initial examination we did find prints from a trainer. Whoever made it must have stood in the pool of blood surrounding the victim's head. The clearest print is between the head and the wall with the writing on it. Find those trainers and I suspect we'll find traces of the victim's blood on the soles," Julian said.

"What size?"

"Small, so possibly a woman's," Julian said.

Higgs was a big bloke, so it couldn't be him. "Thanks, we'll get on to it. We have someone in mind, so I should have something for you later today."

Calladine was thinking of Jade O'Brien. They'd have to pay another visit to Angel Court, but this time they'd be sure to get a warrant first.

* * *

Within the hour, Ruth was back from the depths. "I found something," she told Alice, dumping a storage box on the spare desk. She tapped on Calladine's office window and beckoned to him. He should see this too.

"Have you spoken to Long?" she asked him when he joined them.

"Yes, he doesn't remember a thing. Bloody useless he is."

"Well, you should. I've had a look through his old files and there's a lot in them. Whether you remember or not, there was an investigation of sorts after Agnes Reed died and Millie disappeared. The house was searched, and a number of items taken away." She nudged him. "Bet you didn't know that, did you?"

"Why? Agnes Reed died of a stroke," he said.

"She did, but there was no sign of Millie. The girl simply vanished, didn't even attend the funeral. It's thought the last time she was seen was before her granny was carted off to hospital, on the day she had the stroke."

"I don't recall any suspicion of foul play," Calladine said.

She tapped a folder. "Two years ago, Long spoke to a few folk. After Agnes Reed died it was believed Millie had gone to stay with a cousin of her grandmother's in Liverpool. The milkman went round to Gorse House to collect his money, but no one was in. He thought it odd because the curtains were pulled shut and the place was locked up tight. He told the police, the place was searched, and Forensics gave it a cursory once-over, but there was no evidence that anything untoward had happened to the girl. They did find a letter, however, from a woman called Florence Reed offering to take Millie. She would have been sixteen by then, so, given the letter it's possible that no one looked too hard."

"Owt else in the box?" he asked.

"Stuff that belonged to Millie." She smiled. "After a few months, her form teacher at Leesdon High contacted us and brought in a PE kit belonging to Millie that had been left in her locker."

"How does it help us now?" Calladine asked.

Ruth lifted out the bag. It was made of heavy cotton with a drawstring fastening, the type of thing kids made in needlework. "It contains a pair of shorts, gym shoes, a T-shirt and a hairbrush."

Calladine was just about to pick it up when Ruth slapped his hand. "Gloves!" she said. "We're hoping Julian might get valuable information from this. The hairbrush has strands of blonde hair stuck in the bristles. Millie was blonde. Even after all this time, Julian might still be able to get DNA from them."

"I wonder why we didn't know about this box?"

Ruth shook her head. "Down to Long most likely, you know how sloppy he is. The stuff was brought in after the first investigation, catalogued and stashed in the archive. We don't know that Long even knew about it. But when those bones were found he did do an investigation of sorts and discovered that the granny's cousin, Florence Reed, didn't exist. The letter must have been left to stop people looking for Millie."

"That makes the granny appear the guilty party," Calladine said. "The bag's a good find, something independent of that house that possibly links to Millie. We get DNA from the brush or one of the other items, match it with the blood on the skirt fragment and we know it's her bones that were found."

"No thanks to Long. This box has been here years. When Long investigated those bones, he should have checked."

"I'll speak to him. It's looking like those bones are the girl's. Shame. I wonder how she died."

"We'll probably never know, Tom."

"Anyway, on with something we can get to the bottom of. We need another chat with Jade. Julian found trainer prints on the floor of Becca's flat. They belonged to someone with small feet."

"We search her place?" Ruth asked.

"We'll have to. I've organized a warrant. We can drop the PE bag off on the way," he said.

While Ruth and Calladine had been talking, Rocco was on the office phone. He put down the receiver and looked at both of them. "That was your daughter, sir," he told Calladine. "She tried your mobile but no joy."

Calladine checked, it was on silent. "What did she want?"

"She wouldn't say, but it sounded urgent."

"I'll ring her now. Give me a minute," he told Ruth and hurried off to his office.

CHAPTER 19

Zoe Calladine was in tears. "I didn't even see him, Dad," she sobbed. "It was all too quick. One minute we're strolling through the park, then the next . . . This man chucks some liquid from a bottle into Maisie's pram."

Calladine's stomach knotted in horror. Not . . . What the hell was going on? "Is Maisie all right?"

"She's fine. She's been checked over. It was only water, but I completely panicked. For a few seconds I was terrified it might be acid or something."

"Was Amanda with you?" he asked.

"Yes, but she was a few yards behind, talking on her phone."

Calladine was annoyed. These young women were taking this far too casually, especially Amanda. As FLO she ought to be more on her guard. Perhaps he should have been more honest with them, impressed upon them just how dangerous Lazarov was.

"Did you get a look at him?" he asked.

"Young. Jeans, dark hoodie top and trainers. He had the hood up and pulled well down over his face. After he'd thrown the water, he legged it fast towards the road. Amanda went after him, but he disappeared among the shoppers on the High Street."

First the toy and now this. What was Lazarov's game? Both had been geared to scare, not to harm, but Calladine couldn't be sure what the next incident would bring. "Are you at home now?"

"Too right we are, and I doubt I'll ever leave it again."

"Don't worry, Zoe, we'll sort this. I'll make some enquiries and get the protection beefed up. Try and sit tight until I get back to you, and certainly don't take Maisie outside."

"That could be a problem, Dad. Julian wants to have her tomorrow afternoon. He's planning an outing to the park followed by a trip to the Duggan to show her off."

"Leave Julian to me and relax. That particular outing won't be happening."

A grim-faced Calladine left his office and, without a word to the team, went to find Greco. He knocked on his office door and marched straight in. "I want a safe house organizing for Zoe and her family immediately," he demanded.

"Something's happened?"

"Too bloody right it has. Earlier today someone threw liquid into the pram. Thankfully, it was water — another warning from Lazarov I don't doubt. Next time we might not be so lucky."

"I'll arrange a safe house," Greco said at once. "Amanda Knight can go with them. Will you tell your daughter, make sure she knows what to expect?"

Calladine nodded. "I'm going round there now and I'm not leaving until I know they're safe."

"I'll arrange transport and they can be on their way later today. Once it's done, I'll ring your mobile," Greco said. "Who else knows?"

"No one, just you, me, Zoe and Jo."

"Keep it that way."

"I intend to, but Julian will be a problem," Calladine said.

"Oh, yes. He's the child's biological father and is involved in her life. It might be difficult to keep him out of the loop," Greco said.

Calladine heaved a sigh. "I'll deal with him. Do me a favour, get on to Manchester again, will you? See if you can prise anything else out of them regarding Lazarov. Tell them what's happening, make sure they understand. We're attributing this to him because of the note on that first gift, but we could be wrong, and if we are, we need to know what this is about."

"I'll make some calls, find out all I can. Meanwhile, see to your family, Tom."

Calladine made his way back to his office, picked up his coat and a couple of files. The team, particularly Ruth, were giving him curious looks. "I doubt I'll be back until much later," he told them. "Anything urgent comes up, ring my mobile." He looked at Ruth. "Get that warrant and search Jade O'Brien's flat. If you find the bloodstained trainer, bring her in and speak to her again under caution."

"Don't you want to be involved? It could be the break-through we need," she said.

"You go with Rocco, you're both more than capable," he replied.

"Is everything all right, Tom?" she asked. "You look as if you've just had a shock, and your face has that grey tinge again."

Was it any wonder? Calladine shook his head. "I'm fine," he lied. "I'll speak to you later. Right now, I have something urgent to do and it's personal."

On the way to his car, Calladine rang Ronnie Merrick. "It's okay, I won't be needing you. It's a safe house instead," he said. "I'll be in touch if anything changes."

CHAPTER 20

Ruth and Rocco picked up the warrant from the magistrate on their way to Angel Court. Ruth was preoccupied, worried about Calladine. She'd not seen him look so bad in a while.

"What's up?" Rocco asked her. "You seem distant."

"It's Tom, there's something wrong. He's acting weird, and not saying anything."

"The case probably," he replied.

"There's always a case, Rocco. This is different, more serious. He looks dreadful. Worry doesn't suit him. He won't discuss what it is, so all we can do is be there when he needs us."

"Hope it's nowt serious, like he's sick or something," Rocco said.

Ruth didn't know what to think. He'd been fine the night before when they'd eaten their late tea together. "He'll come round soon enough. You know what he's like."

"How's this Jade likely to react to the visit?" Rocco said.

"Jade is a bit unpredictable, to say the least. We tread carefully. The last thing we want is her losing it with us. She has a temper that hasn't got any better over the years."

"You know her?" he asked.

"Hardly, Rocco, but she was at school the same time as me, so I know her by reputation. She was a bully, didn't care who she hurt. Most kids were scared to death of her, and one of them was Millie Reed."

"Could Jade have killed that girl?" Rocco said.

"It's possible. What happened that afternoon twenty-five years ago is still a mystery, but Jade had been in a fight, that much I'm sure of. Jade hated to lose face, she'll have wanted to come out on top and for everyone to know about it. It's possible that she went back up there, scared the granny, and hurt Millie. Unless Jade chooses to tell us, we'll never know."

"What about Jade's injury?"

Ruth shook her head. "Whatever did the damage didn't kick in for a while. Jade must have been unaware of how ill she was. A slow bleed formed a blood clot . . . it put pressure on her brain and eventually led to her falling unconscious. If Jade did get her own back on Millie, it would have to have been that same day."

"She sounds like a right piece of work."

"Back then she was, Rocco. The entire school was scared of her."

"So who saw Millie last, do we know?"

Ruth shrugged. "Probably her granny. Then she slipped through the net. It happens, Rocco."

"You're saying no one really knows when Millie was last seen?"

"Exactly."

* * *

"Can't you leave the woman alone?" Mary Kershaw grumbled. "How long is this going to go on for? It's not doing Jade any good. You know she's delicate."

Ruth showed her the search warrant. "Delicate or not, we need to search Jade's room. Once we're done, we'll be out of your hair."

"What're you looking for? Jade hasn't done anything."

Ignoring her, the pair headed for Jade's flat and Ruth knocked on the door.

"If you have to do this, then I'll take her for a walk, get her out of the way," Mary said following them. "Jade doesn't like people going through her things."

Jade O'Brien opened the door and immediately tried to close it again, but Rocco stuck his foot in the gap.

"Nothing to worry about, Jade," Mary said. "Come downstairs and wait with me while these have a look round. The sooner they're done, the quicker they're gone."

But Jade was furious. She scowled at them. "I don't want them touching my stuff," she said. "I don't want them in here. Why won't you listen? I've done nothing. You have no right to come in like this."

"I'm afraid you've no choice, Jade," Ruth said.

"Get your coat on," Mary Kershaw told her. "I'll take you for a walk while these two get on with their search."

Looking daggers at them, Jade pulled on a navy puffer jacket, thrust her hands in the pockets and followed Mary out.

Ruth made straight for the bedroom and rummaged around in the wardrobe. She found plenty of shoes but no trainers. Rocco was looking through the cupboards in the kitchenette. "Checked under the sink?" she asked.

"Yep, but there's nothing," he said.

Ruth stood in the centre of the sitting room, her hands on her hips. "She didn't have the things on when she went out just now, did she?"

"No," Rocco said. "I looked, and she put on a pair of wellies."

"This place is tiny, where the hell would she hide a pair of trainers?"

"Given she knew they might incriminate her, she could have chucked them away," Rocco said.

"If she has, we're back to square one." Ruth had a last look round. It hadn't taken them long, but they'd searched everywhere. "You did the kitchen — check the washing machine?" He screwed up his face, he obviously hadn't. "Go on then," she said.

Minutes later, he appeared, grinning broadly. "Bingo! One pair of trainers with blood on the soles. Just what we were looking for." Carefully, he put them in an evidence bag.

"Right. Now for the tricky bit," Ruth said. "We have to take Jade in to interview her."

Rocco looked out of the window. "They're just outside, wandering round the gardens."

"We'll get Mary Kershaw to come," Ruth decided. "Responsible adult and all that. She can organize a solicitor for her, too. If Jade has no explanation for the blood, she'll be staying with us."

Jade and her minder returned, and Ruth told them they were taking Jade to the station for questioning. At once, Jade made a dash for the door, but Rocco was already standing in front of it. Mary tried to calm her but didn't have much luck. Jade really kicked off then, threatening to blacken both Ruth's eyes.

"You behave yourself, Jade," Ruth said firmly, "or Rocco here will put you in handcuffs, it's up to you."

Jade glared at her. "You wouldn't dare. I'll bash your bloody 'ead in." She thrust her face into Ruth's. "I can, you know. I've done it before."

"When was that, Jade? Up at Gorse House or round at your mother's the other night?"

Jade curled her lip. "Both. But I'm a nutter, aren't I, so you can't believe a word I say."

CHAPTER 21

Mary Kershaw sorted a solicitor for Jade, and within the hour, the two of them with Mary faced Ruth and Rocco across a table in one of the interview rooms.

"Jade, we were searching your flat for a particular item. Well, we found it." Ruth raised an eyebrow.

"No idea what you're talking about."

"The trainers in your washing machine," Ruth said, "the ones with blood on the soles?"

"Oh, them." Jade shrugged. "Must have stood in summat."

"Any idea what or where?" Rocco asked.

"No. Could have been anywhere."

"I think it was your mother's place. You stepped in her blood the night she was murdered," Ruth said.

"You're off your head, you. Why would I hurt my mum? She wasn't much cop, but it doesn't mean I've done owt to her."

"We're having the blood on your trainers tested, Jade. If that blood turns out to be your mum's, you're in big trouble."

Jade glanced furtively at Mary and started to cry. "It wasn't me," she insisted. "Okay, I was there, I went to see her. I was angry after I had that argument in the library. I

89

wandered around town for a bit and then thought of going to hers. She was dead when I got there."

Now they were getting somewhere. "You were there," Ruth said. "You have a history of violence and your mother was bludgeoned to death. That's your style, Jade, isn't it? It's what you do."

"No! I've changed. I don't do that anymore." Jade leaned towards Ruth. "I'm not that angry cow from school. I've been ill, and it's changed me."

"Did anyone see you at Heron House, Jade? Did you speak to anyone?" Ruth asked.

"By the time I got to the flat, Johnno was already there. It should be him you're speaking to — not me," she hissed. "He told me to leave, said I should go home and not to say a word. He said he'd keep quiet about it too. He walked me to the bus stop." Jade fell silent. Fixed her eyes unflinchingly on Ruth. This was her version of events and she was sticking to it.

"Why write the word 'sorry' on the wall, Jade?" Ruth asked, deliberately omitting to mention the drawing of the heart. She waited for Jade's response.

Jade shook her head. "What d'you mean?"

"'Sorry' was written in your mother's blood. Was that down to you? Doing the same thing you did all those years ago when you hid Millie's body?"

Jade seemed genuinely puzzled. "No. I wouldn't do anything as weird as that. Anyway, there was nothing on any wall — ask Johnno. And I never hurt Millie that much. I cut her, I think, trying to get that bloody mole off her face." She turned to Mary Kershaw. "What's that cow saying about me? I never hid no body."

"You admit to cutting Millie's face?" Ruth asked.

"I don't know, I can't remember properly. But she did annoy me, I know that."

"Was Johnno with you?" Rocco asked.

Jade shook her head.

"Did you tell him what you'd done?"

"I don't remember, it was too long ago."

Ruth looked at Mary Kershaw who sat in silence, impassive. "I don't believe you. I think you remember very well what happened that day. I think you remember what suits you, what fits in with your version of events." She turned to Mary Kershaw. "Until we clear this up, satisfy ourselves that Becca's death isn't down to Jade, she'll be staying with us."

Mary Kershaw looked horrified. "What? You're going to lock her up? You can't do that. You know how she is."

"We'll only be keeping her while we check out her story," Ruth said. "She'll be comfortable enough and we'll keep a close watch on her." Ruth stood up and went to the door. "One thing, Jade. Did you take your mother's mobile phone that night?"

"No, I didn't see it. Thing's usually glued to her hand, too."

* * *

The pair made their way back to the incident room. "She won't like it," Rocco said.

"Can't be helped. Until we can prove otherwise, Jade O'Brien is our prime suspect," Ruth said. "Get uniform to bring Higgs in. I'm just going to give Tom a ring, make sure he's okay."

Ruth called Calladine's mobile from the privacy of his office.

"Is it urgent?" he said.

"Yep. How are you? And don't say 'fine', cause I know you're not. You left here in a right tizz. So come on, what's happened?"

"I tell you and it goes no further. Lives depend on it, Ruth."

"A bit melodramatic, even for you," she said.

"I'm on my way to a safe house with Zoe and her family. They need to be somewhere they can't be found. Their lives are in danger."

"What on earth's happened?" Ruth said.

"Lazarov. He's threatened them to get at me. I'll sort it but I want them safe first," Calladine said.

"You should have told me. I can help, you know."

"You can help me by keeping this to yourself," he said. "The only people who know are you, me and Greco, so don't go telling the others."

"Okay, but take care. I'm not keen on all this secrecy, and anyway, shouldn't it be you staying in a safe house? It's you Lazarov has the beef with."

"I can't sort it hidden away," he said.

Ruth knew it was no use arguing with him. He had that edge to his voice. He would do as he pleased and not be persuaded otherwise. "D'you want to know what happened with Jade O'Brien?"

"No. I'll be in later, tell me then."

Ruth finished the call, really worried now. Lazarov was a dangerous man. With Zoe and her family out of the way, he'd home in on Tom. As if they didn't have enough on their plates.

There was a knock on the door. Rocco. "Uniform are bringing Higgs in. He wasn't hard to find, bloke was propping up the bar in the Pheasant as usual."

"Get a warrant and have Alice organize a search of his flat. Any footwear found is to go straight to the Duggan. They'll want to check for blood and see if the tread matches the print found in the flat. Meanwhile, we'll speak to him, tell him what Jade told us and hopefully get a result."

"If she told the truth, it could mean that Johnno Higgs is our killer," Rocco said.

CHAPTER 22

For once, Johnno Higgs wasn't drunk, but he was angry. "Second time in as many days. How long will this persecution go on? This time those bastards on the front desk took my boots. What the 'ell they do that for?"

They were back in the interview room where they'd spoken to Jade just an hour before. Ignoring his complaints, Ruth said, "Tell me about the night Becca was murdered."

"It had nowt to do with me."

"But you were there — Jade told us." Ruth saw the look on his face. He was rattled. "And what's more, she told us that when she turned up, her mother was already dead."

"She's a lying, scheming bitch. She'll say anything to save her own skin," Higgs said.

He was so nervous he couldn't even look Ruth in the eye. Even so, she knew a liar when she saw one.

"Jade stood in Becca's blood; we found traces on her footwear. Did you do the same, Johnno? When we examine your shoes, will we find Becca's blood on the soles like we did with Jade's?"

He groaned and thumped the table. "I found her like that. Becca rang me, said she needed some stuff, heroin. I went round and found her lying on the floor, all bashed in and bloody. I didn't kill her — I swear. That's down to someone else."

"You see, Johnno, the problem we have is that this isn't the version of events you gave us before. Then, you said you argued with Becca, now you say she was dead. But you shouted at someone, we have a witness who heard you."

"It was Jade I argued with. Becca was already dead. That's the truth. And I didn't kill her."

"So why argue with Jade?" Ruth asked.

He sat for a minute without replying. Then he looked Ruth in the eye and said, "It's hard not to fight with her. She arrives, sees Becca and flies off the handle, but I managed to calm her down. All I wanted to do was get the hell out of there. Okay, so there was some shouting, but it didn't last long. Me and Jade left together. I walked her to the edge of the estate and saw her on to the bus, then I went back to the Pheasant — there was still time for me to get in a couple of pints before the darts match. I told you that last time I were here."

"And we're checking it out," Ruth said, noting it down on her pad. "Tell me about the word 'sorry' written on the wall. Was that down to you?"

Higgs looked mystified. "I've no idea what you're talking about. Me and Jade both saw that Becca was dead, there was nothing we could do. We had a row, yes, we were in shock, but we just wanted to get the hell out of there as fast as we could. Believe me, neither of us hung around to write on any wall."

"You knew Becca was dead, but you left her there. You didn't tell anyone, didn't ring us. Why was that?" Ruth said.

"Best way, I thought. I didn't reckon you'd believe anything I said, and Jade was terrified you'd lock her up and throw away the key. We just didn't want to get involved. I said we should leave her for someone else to find and Jade agreed."

"Did you turn the heating up in the flat?" Ruth asked.

Again, he looked puzzled. "Heating? No. Becca wouldn't have it on, reckoned it cost too much."

Ruth shook her head. "You and Jade were both in that flat, and neither of you can prove that you didn't kill Becca."

"But can you prove we did?" Higgs asked.

He had a point. They needed more evidence before either of them could be charged. "We are doing tests on some items found in your flat. When they are complete, we'll talk again," Ruth said. "But until then, you stay with us, Johnno."

Higgs's face flushed a dark red. "I've just told you — we didn't kill her. Becca was dead when we got there. What does it take to get that through your thick skulls?"

"Evidence, Johnno, simple as that. Did anyone see you both that night?"

He shook his head and turned to the solicitor. "Look, mate, they've got nowt. I'll go mad if I have to stay in here."

"My client does have a point," the duty solicitor pointed out. "You have nothing solid. If you did, you'd charge him."

Ruth knew he was right. "We're searching his flat. If we don't find anything, we'll let him go." She gathered up her notes and left the room with Rocco, closing the door behind them.

"What d'you reckon?" she asked him.

"Has to be one of them, perhaps both, there isn't anyone else. But while they insist on covering for each other, we won't get anywhere."

Ruth shook her head. "I can't help thinking we're missing something with this case. Something that's staring us in the face, but I just can't work out what."

"Like?"

"I don't know, Rocco. Call it intuition. If neither Jade nor Johnno killed Becca, then someone else was in that flat. What we need is evidence to prove it. We get nothing on Higgs, he'll have to be released. Ring Mary Kershaw and get her to collect Jade. The woman is a liability. No point in hanging on to her while there's still so much doubt."

Back in the incident room, Ruth rang Alice. "Search going okay?"

"Fine, but it's taking a while. The man lives in a pigsty. So far, we've found two pairs of shoes — both trainers — and a pair of wellies. We'll have another look round and drop them off at the Duggan on our way back."

"Thanks. I'll ring Julian, bring him up to date." Ruth disappeared into Calladine's office to make the call. "We've got no evidence that will satisfy the CPS," she told Julian. "Our two main suspects don't deny being in that flat and seeing Becca but maintain they didn't do it. They say she was already dead. I need something definitive, Julian."

"I'll do my best," he said. "My team have been over that flat with a fine-tooth comb and they've found a couple of things that look promising. I told you the floor in that flat was a mess. The sitting room floor was covered in both blood and patches of mud, but someone had trodden the mud into every other room in the place. Due to the heat, it had dried. There was a small footprint behind the body, close to the wall where the person who wrote on it would have stood."

"Yes, you told us. The trainer. How does that help, Julian? The mud you found could have come from the shoes of either Jade or Johnno. We've had a lot of rain lately, it's muddy everywhere."

"This mud contains something interesting — skin and a purple stain from the berries of a small tree found in woodland areas, alder buckthorn. We found nothing similar on the sole of Jade's trainer. We'll check the footwear belonging to Johnno Higgs and I'll let you know."

"I've not heard of that tree," Ruth said. "Do we have a lot of them around here?"

"There are none in Leesdon town," he said. "But there are some up in the wooded areas on the hillsides."

"Find the tree and we might find our killer," Ruth said. "Will you text me a photo of it and we'll keep our eyes peeled." There was a silence. Julian would be wondering if she was really serious. "I've no idea what this tree looks like," she said. "A photo would really help."

"No problem. There was also what we suspect is a gloved thumb print on the wall. Black wool, a polyester mix, we have a couple of fibres."

"A glove print. That could be useful."

"Find them and the person they belong to could be your killer."

"Thanks, Julian, food for thought."

CHAPTER 23

The safe house was a large detached residence not far from the village of Longnor in the North Staffordshire moorland, owned and run by a middle-aged couple, John and Catherine Birch. It was positioned on a hillside and had an excellent view of the only road that led up to it.

"We've done this many times before," John Birch assured Calladine. "They'll be well looked after."

Calladine nodded, but he was still anxious. He walked around, checking each room in turn, until at last he was satisfied. It was a good choice. "Amanda will stay with you," he told Zoe, "and there'll be two plain-clothes officers parked up outside all the time. Anything happens, you tell John — phone them and then me, got it?"

Zoe nodded. "Don't you think this is taking things a bit far, Dad? I mean, a safe house for heaven's sake."

Calladine looked at Zoe and Jo Brandon, her partner. "No, I believe you're in danger, all of you. The toy, the water thrown in Maisie's pram were merely warnings. Until I've sorted the bastard responsible, it will ease my mind to know you're all safe and out of harm's way."

Jo nodded. "I agree with your dad, Zoe. We can't take the risk and if anything did happen, we'd never forgive ourselves."

Zoe didn't look impressed. "We'll need food. We can't expect the Birches to feed us. All I brought was baby milk for Maisie."

"Make a list, one of the officers will see to it."

"You said this was aimed at you, not us. Doesn't that mean you're in danger too?"

She had a point. "I can look after myself," he said. "It's part of my job, and with you safely out of the way I'll be able to sort the problem."

"You don't look well," Zoe said. "You haven't for weeks."

"Today's been a bit full-on, that's all," he said.

"What will you tell Julian?"

"Given what's happened, it'll have to be the truth. It's no good lying to him now."

"I don't want him coming up here, Dad. I couldn't cope with him fussing around."

"Don't worry about that. I won't tell him where you are. The fewer people who know that the better."

Calladine said his goodbyes and returned to his car. He wanted to get back to the station. Ruth was more than capable of holding the fort, but he needed something to distract him.

Kitty rang on his mobile. "Fancy eating later?" she asked. "Nothing fancy, just a bite at mine, we don't have to always do the restaurant thing if you'd prefer something quieter. Just you and me, a takeaway from the restaurant downstairs and a bottle of wine."

He liked Kitty. If it wasn't for the case and now Lazarov round his neck, he'd have been more than happy to see her. But not tonight. He needed time on his own to think. "Sorry, Kitty, the workload is pretty heavy at the moment. Can we leave it till the end of the week?"

She sounded put out. "You're a big disappointment, Tom Calladine. I thought you liked me."

"I do, it's just work. I'll ring you tomorrow, I promise." He finished the call and almost immediately his mobile rang again.

"You're a difficult man to contact, Mr Calladine."

His stomach knotted and his hands froze on the wheel. He knew exactly who it was, the heavy Eastern European accent could belong to no one else. "Lazarov!"

He laughed. "I see why you are a detective. We haven't even met yet."

"That doesn't stop me knowing who and what you are. What d'you want?" Calladine said.

"A chat, that is all."

"We have nothing to discuss."

"You're wrong, we have plenty to talk about, and you will listen," Lazarov said.

"Get lost."

"Wrong move, Mr Calladine. You forget, I can be very persuasive."

"Go near my family again and I'll tear your head off," Calladine shouted.

"Now, now, why all the anger? No harm has come to anyone and it won't if you do as you're told."

Calladine pulled into the side of the road. His mobile was on hands-free but he couldn't concentrate on driving with this going on. "What d'you want from me?"

Lazarov laughed again. "Right now, absolutely nothing. All I'm asking is for you to stay out of my business."

What did he mean? Nothing Calladine was currently investigating had anything to do with Lazarov. "What are you up to?"

"I'm about to launch a new arm of my enterprise in your — how do you say it — neck of the woods. For your own good, you will do nothing to interfere with my plans, do you understand?"

"If it's illegal then I'm going to interfere. It's what I do."

"There's nothing you can do to stop me. I am invisible. Try to find me and you'll fail. This call is untraceable. Railing against me is very short-sighted, Mr Calladine. Think of those in your life you are fond of, your family for example. I do not want us to fall out over this. It's really very simple. From today onward, you work for me, and I'll make sure you are amply rewarded."

"I'm a police officer, for God's sake."

"No, Mr Calladine, you are whatever I decide you are, and right now, you're my right-hand man in Leesworth."

CHAPTER 24

After Lazarov's call, Calladine decided to give the station a miss and go straight home. He should ring it in, at least tell Greco. But that would have to wait until later. He was sickened by Lazarov's confident assumption of his corruptibility, but also afraid of the consequences when he refused to play ball.

Calladine was locking his car when his mobile rang again. Yet another voice that sent a shiver down his spine. As if Lazarov wasn't enough.

"Marilyn," he said. "What d'you want?"

"A word. I won't keep you long. Debra's waiting to hear from you. I know you've had a conversation, so you're aware of the favour I need."

Calladine's head was spinning. He wasn't up to this right now, he still needed to get his head round the Lazarov problem. He said nothing, wondering how he could get out of this.

"It's okay," she said. "I'll be no trouble, I promise. I won't abscond or anything. It's like Debra said, I'll be out on parole, so I'll have to be a good girl."

"I can't talk about this now, Marilyn. It's been a long day and I've still got things to do."

"All I need is a place to stay, Tom. Somewhere the powers that be can find me if necessary. I can't stay in this damn hostel any longer. It's noisy and the food's appalling. You have to help me. I mean, we are family — sort of. Debra is happy with the arrangement and it suits me too. It'll only be for a few weeks."

Weeks! Calladine felt his heart skip a beat. He'd never liked Ray and knew very little about Marilyn, except that she'd had no trouble spending Ray's ill-gotten gains. "Isn't there anyone else you can go to? Don't you have family? What about your sister? I'm sure she'd love to see you."

"My parole conditions say I have to stay within the Greater Manchester area, and my sister isn't local."

"I'm not sure, Marilyn. I've been busy and Ms Weller didn't give me a chance to explain properly."

"You don't want me." She sounded upset. "Fair enough. I'll ring Debra and ask if she can make another arrangement. I'm sorry you feel like this, Tom. I thought things would be different."

Calladine felt a surge of relief. It looked like he was off the hook. He fished in his pocket for the house keys, expecting her to end the call.

"I'll be out in a day or two. I'll ask Debra to pick up Sam for me."

Calladine let his hand drop. His heart sank. "Sam? You can't take him."

"Yes, I can, Tom, he's my dog. You're simply taking care of him for me. But the arrangement was never meant to be permanent."

Calladine had grown fond of the dog, he liked having him around and didn't want to see him dragged off like this. Sam was old and, like him, he didn't do change well.

"Look, let me sleep on it," he said. "I'll speak to Debra tomorrow. We'll leave discussing Sam until then. He's settled with me and he's got one or two problems, arthritic joints for one. He's on medication and it doesn't come cheap."

"He's still my dog, Tom. Wherever I go, he comes with me."

* * *

Despite his problems, a couple of whiskies had Calladine nodding in front of the fire. He woke with a start to the sound of his mobile. He looked around. Sam was fast asleep on the sofa — the ring hadn't even disturbed him. The dog had settled well into his life here. No way could he just let Marilyn walk away with him. He'd have to think of something, and quick.

"What is it?" he asked.

"Rocco here, sir. There's been an incident on the Hobfield."

Nothing new there, so why bother him? "It's bloody late. Couldn't you get a couple of uniforms to sort it?"

"No, sir, it's a shooting. A couple of teenagers. They're dead."

Calladine sighed. The day just kept throwing punches at him. Despite feeling as low as he could ever remember, Calladine had no choice, he'd have to attend. "Natasha and her crew on site?"

"Yes, and her first observations are that it looks like an execution. Both lads have been tied to chairs and have been shot between the eyes. I did try Ruth, but I couldn't raise her."

"She'll be seeing to the little lad. Text me the address and give me ten minutes."

CHAPTER 25

The shooting had taken place on the third floor of Heron House. Not so far to climb as the O'Brien flat, nonetheless, it was still a breathless Calladine who joined the swelling ranks of police and forensic investigators.

"We've not had anything like this in a while," Natasha said when she saw him. "Two young men, no more than twenty I'd say. No identification and no mobile phones. Both have been strapped to chairs with gaffer tape, gagged and shot at point-blank range between the eyes." She pointed. "Doesn't look much here but it's a hell of a mess at the back where the bullets exited. Forensics will examine the wall to find the bullets."

Calladine pointed to one of the lads. "I know him. He's Billy Downs, lives a few floors up with his dad. He's been seen knocking about with Johnno Higgs of late."

"Well, at least we know Higgs has nothing to do with this, he's been in custody up until an hour ago," Rocco said. "What about the other one?"

"No idea. He's a new one on me." Calladine looked around the room. Apart from the chairs the lads were tied to, there was a table and a battered old sofa. He nodded at a door to one side. "What's in there?"

"It's supposed to be a kitchen, but it's been stripped out. According to a woman further up the deck, this flat has been empty for weeks, and folk have simply helped themselves to whatever fittings they fancied."

"Is there a tenant at the moment?" Calladine asked.

Rocco shook his head. "As far as I'm concerned, this entire estate should be razed to the ground. That'd sort most of the problems in this town."

But Calladine wasn't listening. He scoured the room for anything that would give them a clue. There was white powder under the table, and some had been scattered over the two lads.

"Cocaine, I suspect." Natasha had followed his gaze. "A falling out among dealers perhaps? There's more of that mud on the floor, too, same as in the O'Brien flat."

Two facts that gave Calladine a bad feeling. Dealing hadn't been an issue on the Hobfield lately. It still went on, but it was low-key. This had all the hallmarks of a new head man making his presence known, and that could only mean Lazarov. He was getting rid of the opposition. As for the mud, he'd no idea what that meant.

Someone called out to him. It was Julian. "We'll do a quick sweep, seal the place and return tomorrow to do a more detailed forensic search." He nodded at the bodies. "I'm thinking a new drugs war." Calladine nodded. "The last thing we need."

But Calladine said nothing.

"I can't raise Zoe. Has she gone away?" Julian said.

Calladine hadn't yet decided what to tell Julian and was caught on the hop. "Er, yes, they've gone to a friend of hers for a few days. Show off the little one, have a bit of a break." Not a bad off-the-cuff explanation for a tired bloke who just wanted his bed. Julian even cracked a rare smile.

"So, why doesn't she answer her mobile?"

Calladine shrugged. "Her friend lives out in the sticks, probably a bad signal. I shouldn't worry."

Deep in thought, he watched while Julian went back to collecting samples. A problem swerved, but there would be a next time. Sooner or later, he'd have to tell him the truth.

"I'll get them back to the morgue, Tom," Natasha said. "You'll tell the Downs boy's family?"

Calladine nodded. He didn't fancy a conversation with Phil Downs, but he had no choice, he should know his lad was dead. He turned to Rocco. "I want Higgs to stay in custody until I've spoken to him. He might know what's going on." He looked again at the bodies. "We need an ID on that one. I'll ask Downs if he knows him."

There was nothing else he could do here, so he trudged up the stairs to the Downs flat and banged on the door. The man who opened it didn't look happy.

"D'you know what bloody time it is? What's the little sod done now?"

Obviously well used to the antics of his son. "If you mean Billy, I'm afraid he's been murdered," Calladine said bluntly. "Happened this evening, a few floors down." He knew there was just the two of them in this flat and they frequently came to blows. Calladine also knew that uniform visited often due to the neighbours' complaints. Even tonight, Phil Downs was sporting a freshly blackened eye.

"Is that what I heard?" he asked. "It sounded like a gunshot, but I put it down to a car backfiring. What happened? Who'd he upset?"

"We don't know. He's been seen hanging about with Johnno Higgs, but did Billy mix with anyone else?"

"He never told me much. You know as well as I do what it's like round 'ere. Johnno was a dealer of sorts and like a fool Billy helped him. He said they'd been getting grief lately, but he never said who from."

"You sure? He never let a name slip, or told you who him and Johnno were up against?"

"He told me nowt and that's how I liked it. Know too much, say too much is a sure way to get beaten up or killed round 'ere. Look what just happened to our Billy."

The man didn't appear too surprised or upset at the news of his son's death. "There were two of them, your Billy and another young bloke about his age. Any idea?" Downs shook his head. Calladine was weary. He didn't have the patience to prise information from a man who'd do his level best to avoid telling him anything useful. He handed him his card. "You find out more, let us know."

He made his way back down the steps. He was about to get into his car and make for home when his mobile rang. It was Lazarov. He sounded angry.

"You've found them. Now you know what I am capable of. The shootings are merely a warning, Mr Calladine, so take heed. I will not tolerate people getting in my way. Those young men were foolish, refused to recognize the new order. Do not make the same mistake. I am running the town now, and things are about to change."

"You murdering—"

Lazarov laughed. "Your job is simple. You will put a stop to the turf war. Tell the opposition to back off before more people lose their lives."

Just like that. Did the man think he had a magic wand up his sleeve? "How am I supposed to do that? The turf war, as you call it, is your doing."

"I buy the merchandise and organize distribution. I do not rid the market of competition. That is your job. Make sure anyone who gets overly ambitious knows the penalty for interfering in my business."

He finished the call. Calladine was furious with himself for not recording the conversation. He had presumed the murders were down to Lazarov and that conversation had just proved him right. The man wasn't shy about confessing, but then he didn't expect to get caught. Calladine wanted Lazarov behind bars, but first he'd need to catch him.

CHAPTER 26

Day Four

"I believe there was a bit of excitement on the Hobfield last night," Ruth said to Calladine the following morning.

"Later, Ruth. Too much to think about right now. First, I want another word with Higgs."

Ruth shook her head. "We'll have to find him first, and after what's happened on the Hobfield, what's the chance of that?"

"Get uniform on it, look in all his usual haunts. He knew those two victims and I'm short of a name."

"What's eating you?" she said. "If there's something wrong on that estate, I should know about it. You're not a one-man band, you know."

"Sorry," he said. "Lot on my plate — Zoe, Marilyn, Lazarov . . . where do I start? And don't say a word to the others about Zoe. Greco knows, but no one else does."

He saw the look. She wasn't happy. "You should trust me more, Tom. I can help you, take on some of the burden. It is my job after all."

"Zoe isn't, she's personal."

"Lazarov is work," she said pointedly.

"Marilyn's becoming a pain too," he said. "I've been asked to babysit her for a while. God knows why, we never liked each other. But she's threatening to take Sam if I refuse."

"That's just cruel. You love that dog. Look, we could have lunch later, you can have a good whine and we'll put together a plan."

"Let's see how the morning goes."

"Julian's been on," she said. "There's blood on a pair of Johnno's shoes but no mud, same as Jade's."

"So they stood in the blood, but whoever trampled the mud into the flat must have gone in later," Calladine said.

"They too will have seen the body and not reported it," Ruth noted. "What do we do now? We don't have anything else on either of them, only their footwear. Neither has a good-enough motive for killing Becca. Johnno thought she was a pain, but he's never been violent towards her in the past."

"Fair enough. He's a small-time dealer, and I don't see him as a murderer, not got the bottle."

"I think you're right, and I don't think Jade is either. Is she really capable of battering her own mother to death and keeping quiet about it? Maybe a long time ago, but not any-more. Not that that helps us any."

"She is unpredictable though. That type might do anything."

The sound of the office phone stopped any further con-versation. It was one of the uniforms who'd been out looking for Higgs. They'd found him wandering through the park and were bringing him in.

"Higgs has been found. This time, he's got some straight-talking to do," Calladine said.

"Am I allowed to join you?" Ruth said.

"Don't be daft, I always welcome your input. I'm in a bad mood, that's all."

Within the hour, Higgs had been processed and was wait-ing in one of the interview rooms. Calladine and Ruth sat down opposite him.

"Tell me about the takeover on the Hobfield," Calladine said at once.

"Don't know what you're on about," Higgs said.

"Oh yes you do. I'm disappointed in you, Johnno, you should have told us about this before. There's a new dealer, head man, call him what you will, and he's throwing his weight around. I want a name before anyone else ends up dead."

Calladine was determined to get Higgs to say what he knew about Lazarov.

"You've got it wrong, there's nowt happening. I'm being upfront, Mr Calladine." Higgs sounded genuine enough, but he kept his eyes on the floor.

"No you're not, you're lying. I want a name."

"If I knew, I'd tell you, but I don't. All the dealing that goes down around here is small-time, been the same for ages."

"I don't believe you. You're scared." Calladine leaned forward. "I can understand that, Johnno. I'd be scared too. But if you give me a name, I can get him off the streets."

Higgs said nothing.

"A couple of your mates were shot last night. One of them was Billy Downs — right between the eyes, didn't have a chance. It could be you next."

Higgs shook his head. "I don't know owt about no shooting."

"Someone is getting rid of the old order," Calladine said.

"Look, what d'you want me to say?" Johnno shouted. "I can't give you information I don't have."

Calladine was getting impatient, they'd be here all day at this rate. "Who are you afraid of? Give me a name, Johnno. You aren't leaving until I get one."

Finally, Johnno Higgs looked him in the eye. "Look, I don't know no name. I've just heard talk of some bloke being around. Got a foreign accent and plenty of muscle to call on, so they say. I decided to back off for a while, see what happened. Billy and his mate were braver, they weren't ready to give up. I did my best to warn them, but they weren't up for listening."

Foreign accent. Lazarov, had to be. So this was the business he spoke about — drug dealing. "How long has he been around?"

"I don't know. Doesn't seem to be any takeover. All I know is what this bloke told Billy and he told me, that there'd be plenty of dope to go round. Cheap, too. They plan to rope in the kids, have them going all over, delivering stuff."

Calladine nodded. "See, that wasn't hard, was it, Johnno?"

"I said that's what Billy told me," Higgs emphasized. "It wasn't what I saw happening."

"And Becca intended to ask these new people for something the night she was killed?" Calladine said.

Higgs looked down again. "Reckon so. I know she had no money to speak of. I'd have done her a freebie — she was an old mate — but I had no dope to give her, no money neither. Billy said the new lot were selling cheap, but they weren't giving it away. If she couldn't pay and started with the screaming and fighting . . . that could've been what got her killed."

Calladine nodded, but he doubted that the same people killed Becca and shot the lads — totally different MO. Apart from which, what had happened to Becca looked personal to him. There was that strange message for a start. "Where's he living, this new bloke?"

"No idea," Higgs said. "Billy only ever spoke to him on the phone, said he were foreign and that he had muscle. All over the Hobfield the other night they was."

"Which night, Johnno?" Calladine asked.

"Tuesday, the next night after Becca got it."

"Anything else you can tell me? It could save your life."

Higgs shook his head.

Calladine guessed he'd given them all the information he had. The problem was, what would happen to him if he was released? "You're free to go, Johnno, but it might be an idea to lie low for a while, until we've put this new drugs thing to bed. I've got your mobile number. If I need you again, I'll ring." He looked him in the eye. "I ring, you answer, got that? If I need to interview you, I'll send a car."

"Thanks, Mr Calladine."

"Before you go, what was the name of the lad Billy hung around with?"

"Daz. Darren Heap. Lives in Lowermill."

"Lived," Calladine corrected. "He was shot along with Billy. Make sure you keep out of sight once we release you, Johnno. I don't want to find you with a bullet in your head."

* * *

Calladine and Ruth went back to the incident room no closer to finding Becca O'Brien's killer. Given that what happened to her wasn't connected to the shootings, that gave them a problem.

"We've not got the manpower," Calladine told Ruth. "If Higgs is right, then this drugs thing is big. I'll have a word with Greco, see what he can come up with."

Ruth handed him a printout. "Here, I got this from the files. It's a photo of Lazarov. Now you know what he looks like."

Calladine saw a heavy-set, wide face, cropped dark hair and neatly trimmed beard. "Ugly-looking bugger, isn't he? Is there anything else? Information about his whereabouts for instance?"

"No, nothing on him that's recent," she said.

Rocco came over to them. "Julian's been on. He's got some results and wants to discuss them with you."

"Okay, we'll go and see Julian later. First, I'll have that word with Greco."

CHAPTER 27

Greco was perturbed about the events of the previous night, and rightly so. "Manchester believe Lazarov to be holed up in their area with the intention of staying out of sight."

"They're wrong. He's here in Leesworth and killing people. This operation must have taken some setting up. Sorting the kids who'll deliver the stuff for a start, plus the people who organize them. Lazarov can't have built a web like that overnight. I don't believe Manchester are oblivious to what's going on."

"Well, that's what they maintain. They had a tip-off a few weeks ago that he was living quietly with a woman in the Fallowfield area of the city. Manchester Major Incident Squad raided the address but he wasn't there. The woman said she'd no idea where he'd gone and knew nothing about his reputation." Greco reached for a file. "One Maggie Cox. She works at the infirmary."

"Nurse? Doctor?" Calladine asked.

"Physio, it says here. What someone like her was doing with Lazarov is anyone's guess," Greco said.

"Providing him with an alibi, an address to use while he gets his business together, who knows?" Calladine said. "But one thing's for sure, my team will be stretched to cover both cases. The O'Brien case alone is a head-scratcher, without the added complication of a new drugs war on our doorstep."

"I'd speak to Long, but his team are snowed under too," Greco said.

Calladine was losing patience. If he couldn't get help, it was hopeless. "We need more bodies from somewhere, the background gathering alone will be a full-time task. We're going to need a full breakdown — who's working for Lazarov and their movements during these last weeks, plus alibis for last night. Then there's the local youth he's using as runners. They need rounding up and questioning."

Greco's silence unnerved Calladine. He waited, watching the immaculately dressed man behind his oh-so-neat desk. His expression gave nothing away, but Calladine could picture the cogs in his brain whirring with logical precision.

"We could split the team into two halves," Greco said at last. "You lead one and continue with the O'Brien case and I'll lead the other and deal with Lazarov."

It could work. Greco was a good detective. If anyone could catch Lazarov, it was him. "Okay, that suits me. Who d'you want to work with?"

More silence. "Ruth," he said finally, "and you take Rocco. Alice can work on the background stuff for both cases."

Not a solution Calladine was keen on. Ruth was his right arm, and he wasn't used to working without her. "We've got Joyce, too," he said hopefully, reminding Greco about their information assistant. "Don't forget her, she's damned good, knows her stuff."

"Alice and Joyce then, between them they should be able to get the background info we need, chase up alibis and the like," Greco said.

Calladine pulled a face. "You really want Ruth to work with you?"

Greco smiled. "I know you have a special relationship but she's not your personal property, you know. Ruth's a good officer and I need her with me. She knows the area well and has a way with people, both assets I'm sadly lacking in."

He was nothing if not honest. "Sorry, Stephen. It's just that I'm so used to having her at my side. But needs must and all that."

Greco checked the time. "I'll leave you to tell them and we'll make a start after lunch. We'll chase up Maggie Cox, the forensics found in that flat and go from there."

Calladine left him to it. Given the shortage of manpower, it wasn't a bad plan. It was just that losing Ruth made him ill at ease.

* * *

"Should I be flattered that he wants me to work with him?" Ruth said.

Calladine, helping himself to a free copy of the local paper from the stand in the canteen, made a face. "Please yourself. But you know what he's like. Most likely he'll drive you to drink before you're through."

Ruth ignored the jibe. She thought Greco was okay, and that everyone misunderstood him, particularly Calladine. Greco was a fair man. Ruth eyed the lunch menu and sighed. "Doesn't get any better, does it? I thought that by now there'd be more of a move towards healthy eating. All I see is one measly plate of salad."

Calladine took no notice, he was immersed in the newspaper headline. "The Leesworth Hoard's coming back. They've plastered all the details across the front page — dates, where it will be on display . . . an invite to every bloody reprobate in the area."

"Greco told me about that. It'll be fine, it's coming complete with its own security."

"Just so long as it doesn't involve us," Calladine said.

"The Hoard was found round here, and here it should stay," she said. "D'you know, Jake had to take twenty

116

teenagers on a trip to London to see it. The school paid but the expense was crippling. Now they can see it for free right on their doorstep."

"Lot of fuss about a load of old jewels. Council should sell it, fill the coffers, do some well-needed repairs to the local roads."

"Philistine. It's Leesworth's history. It's important, never mind selling it off."

"Leesworth's history is woollen mills, poverty and bloody hard work. That gold was left buried in the hills by the Celts on their way to wherever they came from hundreds of years ago. I'm sure they intended to come back for it. If they had, we wouldn't have the problem."

Ruth ignored the remark. "What're you having? I'll have the salad, minus that ham, it looks a bit fatty."

"Sod that. I'm having pie, chips and mushy peas with loads of gravy."

Ruth pulled a face. "Don't you ever consider what all that rubbish is doing to your body?"

"Nope. Better things to stress about. Anyway, you've no room to talk. You were the one who bought me a chippy tea, remember?"

They sat at a table by the window, not that the car park was much of a view, but Ruth liked to watch the birds. "I've put a feeder over there on a branch of that tree." She pointed. "The blue tits and nuthatches really like it." She watched Calladine tuck into his plate of stodge and sighed. "You need taking in hand."

"What's a nuthatch?" he asked.

She smiled. "A small woodland bird with a pointy beak. I always think they look like little darts."

"And there's some over there." He nodded.

"Yes, those trees also border the park." She smiled. "You should open your eyes, give nature a look in."

"Birdwatching's your thing. I've not got the energy for watching owt but telly these days," he said.

"It doesn't take energy, just a pair of eyes. It's relaxing, and you need something to take your mind off work. So, I've got Greco, who're you working with?"

"I think it's more a case of Greco's got you," he said. "I'm working the O'Brien case with Rocco. Alice will cover all our research needs with Joyce."

Ruth laughed. "She'll love that. You know what she's like, much prefers the sharp end does Alice."

"She'll cope, we'll all have to."

"Oh dear, you are feeling sorry for yourself," she said. "C'mon then, what's up?"

"Lazarov wants me dead," he said simply. "So make sure you get him before he gets me."

"The man really has got to you," she said.

"He's threatened my family, Ruth, and now he imagines he can go around this town killing people as he thinks fit." He pushed the half-eaten plate of food to one side. His appetite had vanished. "He's told me to back off chasing him and sort out his competition instead. I'm to ensure he has a clear run at this new drug-supply business of his."

"He rang you?" she said.

"Yes, that's another thing, how come he knows my mobile number?"

Ruth held out her hand. "Give it here."

Calladine passed his phone over.

"Mind if I keep this? I'll get Roxy to take a look."

"But I need it. What do I do now?" he said.

"You get issued with another one. It's no big deal, Tom. And I promise not to look at anything personal."

"Personal? I should be so lucky," he said.

"You've put Zoe somewhere safe, haven't you?" Ruth asked.

"Yes, but I've got other family, and friends." He smiled at her. "And Lazarov isn't all of it, there's also Marilyn. She's threatened to take Sam back if I don't let her stay with me."

"I don't understand what she's doing out of prison in the first place. She killed Ray — she planned it, took the poison with her on a visit, for goodness' sake. What does it take?"

"She's done a deal," Calladine said. "It's the only explanation that makes any sense. She spouted a load of crap about killing him out of fear, but that's not true. Marilyn's never been scared of anything, and particularly not Ray."

"What sort of deal?"

"No doubt she told them where to find money never recovered, about jobs Ray did that were never cleared up. You know the stuff. Marilyn must have a wealth of information on Ray that the police would be happy to get hold of."

"But why you?" Ruth asked.

"There's no one else," he said. "She has to stay local for a while. Long-term she intends to go to Cumbria, be with her sister."

"And Sam?"

Calladine shook his head. "I can't lose him, Ruth. Sam's what keeps me sane."

CHAPTER 28

Greco negotiated the heavy traffic in central Manchester, heading for the address in Hulme that they'd been given for Maggie Cox. "That's the street there," Ruth said. He indicated and checked in the mirror for the two vans following them — backup in case of trouble. Lazarov was a killer. For all they knew, he could be here, and Greco wasn't taking any chances.

He slowed down to take the turn-off and a bus behind them blasted its horn. "Busy place," he said. "No one gives an inch."

"Not like Leesdon," Ruth said. "We can park up here, it's only a few metres further along. There's plenty of room for the vans over there."

They were on a road of red-brick terraced houses. Behind, four grey tower blocks rose to meet the grey sky.

"And I thought Leesdon was bad. I don't envy our colleagues who police this little lot," Greco said. "Let's get on with it." He got out of the car, straightened his tie and smoothed his blond hair.

Ruth grinned. "All neat and tidy."

Greco gave her a small, tight smile. "Can't help it. I'm afraid it's just the way I am."

"I'm not being critical, it's just that you're so different from Tom. I mean, let's face it, the man's a first-class slob. I'm always having to sponge the remnants of his lunch from his clothes." She laughed.

Greco glanced briefly at his own pristine white shirt. He looked horrified. "He's a damn good detective though."

"A damn good detective who looks as if he's got the world on his shoulders right now," she said.

Maggie Cox's house was near the end of the row. Greco rang the bell and they waited. After a few minutes, a young dark-haired woman came to the door and smiled at them.

Greco showed her his badge. "We'd like a word about Andrei Lazarov."

The smile disappeared, and she backed into the hallway. "Come in, it's better if no one overhears us. Andrei was here for a couple of weeks, but he upset the neighbours. One night he got violent with one of them, lost it completely, so I told him to go. I haven't seen him since."

"Were you aware that he's a wanted criminal?" Ruth asked.

She shook her head. "Not at first, but after a while I did suspect. I knew he wasn't exactly whiter than white but I'd no idea you lot were looking for him, until the house was raided. After that I knew exactly what he was."

"D'you know where he's gone?" Greco asked.

"No, and I haven't heard from him either. No call, no text, nothing."

"When did he leave?" Ruth asked.

"About a month ago, after he attacked my neighbour. We had a row and he left. He didn't say where he was going and frankly, I didn't care. I'd had enough."

"What was your relationship with Lazarov?" Greco asked.

"For a while we were lovers," she said. "We met in a club in Huddersfield a few months ago. I was with friends at a birthday party. We got on, he rang me a few times and things went from there."

121

"You invited him to stay with you?" Ruth asked.

"Andrei said he had business around here and asked if I could put him up. I had no reason to refuse, I liked him."

"And you're sure you haven't heard from him?" Greco said.

"Positive. It was good while it lasted, but Andrei has a temper on him. The way he lost it with the neighbour, it shocked me."

"Do you know any of his associates? Did anyone ever come here to see him?" Greco asked.

"No, but people did ring him. He'd often speak to them in his own language, Bulgarian. I never pried but I got the feeling from his tone that all wasn't well." She stared at them both. "What's happened? Andrei hasn't been hurt, has he?"

"No, Ms Cox, quite the reverse," Greco said. "Did he leave any of his belongings behind?"

"That's how I knew he wouldn't be back. He took absolutely everything with him."

"Do you have his address in Huddersfield?" Greco asked.

"He said that up until moving in with me, he'd been living with his mother in Lockwood."

That was consistent anyway. Greco nodded. "Okay, that'll do for now, but I may want to talk to you again."

Ruth returned to the car while Greco, somewhat relieved, had a quick word with the team in the backup vans. They'd had a wasted journey, but had Lazarov been in that house, things could have gone very differently. The man was a killer, and he wouldn't have hesitated to fight his way out.

"On the way back we'll call in at the Duggan, see if Professor Batho has anything for us," Greco said, climbing in beside Ruth.

"Call him Julian, not professor, we all do," she said. "He's big-headed enough as it is."

* * *

"There was a large amount of blood and brain tissue splattered over the wall behind where the victims were seated — the bullet exit wounds. There were no footprints or fingerprints to follow up," Julian said.

"What about the bullets?" Greco asked.

"We managed to retrieve both bullets from the wall. They were fired from the same gun. Find it and I should be able to match the striations to the barrel," Julian said.

"We need proof," Ruth said. "Something that puts Lazarov in that flat and the gun in his hand."

Greco shook his head. "Julian can't give you what he hasn't got."

"There was something else. I was just coming to it." Julian glanced up to the clock on the wall. "Tom will be here shortly. He should hear this too."

"Tom isn't part of this investigation," Greco said firmly.

"The evidence I've found might change that," Julian said.

"What evidence? You just ran through it and basically, you've got nothing that helps. What about the tape used to bind them? Wasn't there anything on that?"

Julian shook his head. "No, there are no prints on the tape — I presume the killer wore gloves. However, I did find something."

Julian had that look on his face, the one that said he was about to show his hand and what he had in it was a winner. "Mud," he said finally. "The floor of that flat was covered in it."

"There's spare land at the side of the Hobfield, it's a quagmire. It could have come from there in both instances," Ruth said.

"It didn't. The mud found in both the O'Brien flat and the one where the shootings took place were from the same site, they both had the same make-up."

"Mud's mud, isn't it?" Ruth shrugged.

"No, this mud contained berry skin and juice from the fruit of a particular tree. A tree not found on the Hobfield."

This was totally unexpected. "I don't understand the similarities," Ruth said. "The two cases are very different — Becca was beaten, the two lads were shot. The killer fought with Becca; the lads were killed in an organized, clinical way. Finding berry juice in both places says there has to be a connection."

Julian shrugged. "I didn't say there wasn't. Just that the same mud was left in both flats."

CHAPTER 29

Ruth didn't know what to make of it, nor did Greco. "I read the report on the mud found on the floor of the O'Brien flat," he said. "Do we know exactly where it came from?"

"Not yet, but I've got people collecting samples from likely locations," Julian replied.

"It can't have been trodden in on the killer's footwear, sir," Ruth said. "We examined both suspects' shoes in the O'Brien case, found blood, but no mud. Whoever trod it in must have entered that flat after Becca was killed."

Calladine and Rocco arrived. "Julian's got some interesting results," Ruth said to them. "We're still trying to work out what it means."

"I'll discuss the results that pertain only to the O'Brien case shortly," Julian said. "But first, there's something that is important to both cases and that I admit has me puzzled."

They all sat down at the table.

"Mud was found on the floor of the flat where the lads were shot, the same mud had been found in the O'Brien flat. I tested samples from each place and found them both to contain purple juice and skin from the berry of the alder buckthorn tree."

Calladine and Rocco took a moment or two to process this. Calladine had no immediate explanation. Did it mean the cases were connected after all? But how? Had the shooter also been in Becca's flat after she'd been beaten to death? Perhaps it was the killer returning later to check on his handiwork. Neither Johnno nor Jade had killed Becca, so it was possible. Or was it simply a matter of cross-contamination? "There might have been mud on the deck," Calladine said to Julian. "Perhaps some of it was trampled into that flat where the lads were shot."

"We checked that and found none," Julian said.

Greco nodded. "Well, if the killer or killers walked wherever these trees are and got mud on their footwear or clothing, it means they are local." He turned to look at Julian. "I'd like a list of all the locations you're aware of where these trees are found."

Julian nodded.

"The idea of Lazarov being somewhere round here terrifies the bloody life out of me," Calladine said. He turned to face Greco. "And if he is, can I suggest you find out where's he's staying at the earliest? Perhaps then I'll be able to sleep at night."

"We're doing all we can," Greco said. "I want the man found every bit as much as you." He turned to Julian. "Is that it? Only we should get on."

"Tests are ongoing. I get anything else, you'll be the first to know. I'll text you the list of locations."

* * *

Something was wrong. Calladine didn't believe the cases were connected, they couldn't be. But Julian had found evidence. He needed time to think it through, but that wasn't now.

"Do you think there's a link between these cases, Tom?" Julian asked.

Calladine shook his head. "It's possible I suppose, but how likely is it that both Becca O'Brien's killer and whoever

126

shot the lads both went for a stroll in the woods before they did the deed? Anyway, I'm still convinced that Becca's murder was personal." He rubbed his head. "I'm in no shape to work it out at the moment. Too much crap in my life."

"Sorry, Tom, you're finding it a hard grind, I can see that. You look like you could do with a break," Julian said.

Calladine gave a hollow laugh. "No chance of that. This little lot needs sorting before I can even consider it."

"Well," said Julian, changing the subject, "I have results for you regarding the Reed girl. The clothing, footwear and brush we found in her PE bag has yielded some DNA. It is a match to what we extracted from the blood on the skirt remnants found with the bones."

"Thanks, Julian," Calladine said. "That means those bones do belong to Millie Reed." He saw the look — Julian had more to say.

"Not necessarily. All it really proves, Tom, is that Millie's blood got on to that skirt, not that the bones are hers."

Calladine had had enough. Was nothing straightforward anymore? "Can't you test the bones themselves in that case? Surely you can get DNA from them?"

"Yes, but it would be expensive and take time. When they were originally found along with the other items, it was presumed that on the balance of probability they did belong to the girl. Foul play might have been suspected but there was no one to charge, the grandmother was dead. And unlike now, we didn't have any of the Reed girl's DNA for a comparison, so things were left as they stood."

Calladine was thinking hard, trying to work out if it was important to know now. His instincts told him it was, but he wasn't sure why. But was a hunch, a feeling in his gut, good-enough reason to authorize the expensive tests?

"Do the tests, Julian," he decided. "Find out if the DNA you got from the PE bag is a match for those bones."

"Will Greco be okay with the expense?" Julian asked.

"We'll keep it to ourselves for now."

CHAPTER 30

Greco and Ruth were back in the car and about to drive off when Ruth got a call from Alice. "A lead on the second shooting victim, Darren Heap," Ruth told Greco. "A young woman has reported him missing. We should talk to her, see what he told her about the drug business on the Hobfield. She works in the greengrocer's in Lowermill, Alice is texting the address."

"Lowermill?" Greco asked.

"Through Leesdon, up the hill and then take the right-hand fork."

He nodded. "I think we looked at a house there."

"You're thinking of leaving Oldston?" Ruth asked.

"It would make sense. It's not far but the traffic at peak times is dreadful."

Ruth nodded. "Provided Grace is happy to move, you should go for it."

"What d'you think about the forensics Julian's turned up?" he asked her.

"Calladine's convinced the cases aren't linked and I tend to agree with him. They are too different — one a beating, the other shootings — and they were killed for different reasons.

Becca O'Brien's murder is only loosely connected to drugs. Maybe she annoyed her dealer so much he thumped her one, who knows?" Ruth said. "And then there's the mystery of the word 'sorry' written on her wall."

"Different cases then, as we thought," Greco agreed. "But that doesn't explain Julian's forensics."

"Those trees are a puzzle. The berry juice suggests that whoever the killer is, they were up in the woods soon before the killings."

"Could someone be camping out up there?" Greco asked.

"It's possible, but the weather's not the greatest at the moment," she said. "And if there were two different killers, why would they both be there?"

"Can you walk from the hillside down to the Hobfield?" Greco asked.

"Yes, there's a pathway on to the road, then you take the canal towpath to the back of the estate beyond the fence," she said.

"Fence?"

"It's not difficult to get over and there are gaps in places where the kids have taken the metal to weigh in. If that's what happened, it does suggest a killer who knows the area well," Ruth said.

"Organize for Julian's people to take a look along the towpath and pay particular attention to the fence and a gap someone might have used," Greco said.

It was market day in Lowermill and half of Leesworth was out shopping. She heard Greco tut at the slow-moving traffic and his fingers tapped on the dash. A man who was easily irritated. She wondered how he coped with a houseful of small children. He and Grace had an infant. Then there were Grace's daughter Holly and Greco's Matilda. Ruth was driving and the High Street was busy, but she knew exactly where to find a parking space.

She pointed to a row of shops. "The greengrocer's is just over there. We'll stick the car round the back."

"Let's make this quick," Greco said. "I have a photo for her to look at. We get a positive ID, ask a few questions, then go on to the victim's family. They should be told what's happened."

Josie Hardwick was serving behind the counter when they entered the shop. She took one look at the detectives and her face turned pale.

"We're here about your friend," Greco said.

"What friend? What's happened?"

"Darren," he said quietly.

She folded her arms and looked away. "What's he been up to now? You're not ordinary coppers, you're plain clothes — CID — and that means trouble."

The customer she'd been serving went out, leaving the shop empty. Ruth took the liberty of shutting the door and putting up the closed sign.

Greco held out his mobile so she could look at the image. "Is this him, Ms Hardwick?"

The girl gave it a glance and nodded.

"We're very sorry, Josie," Ruth said. "Darren has been killed, murdered. Are you up to helping us by answering a few questions?"

The girl burst into tears. "Poor Darren. I warned him. I was always telling him not to get involved with those losers."

"Who d'you mean?" Ruth asked.

"Johnno Higgs and Billy. They're not really bad, just can't get anything right. I knew there'd be trouble when Billy said he'd been told there was new people on the estate trying to take over. Word was the man running the new outfit wanted the three of them to work for him, but Johnno said they should ignore the offer, carry on as they always had. He told Darren not to worry, that he'd sort him out."

"Very brave of him," Ruth said. "D'you know what this new boss is called?"

She shook her head. "Darren never told me his name, just that he was foreign. I'm not sure that he knew. Johnno told them everything would be fine so long as they didn't attract too much attention or try to muscle in on the new guy's customers."

"They were selling drugs?" Greco asked.

"Johnno's been selling drugs for as long as I can remember. He always has someone different to help him. He's an idiot, all he's good for is pissing folk off."

"This new man, are you sure you don't know who he is?"

"No, but he threatened the three of them, told them to back off, leave the dealing in Leesworth to him or there'd be trouble."

"I take it they didn't comply," Greco said.

"I've no idea. I didn't get involved, but I did warn Darren."

"Does Darren have any family?" Ruth asked.

"No, he lives with me. His dad did one when he was a kid, and his mother died a few years back."

"Thanks, Josie, you've been very helpful," Ruth said.

"What'll happen — you know, about the funeral and such?"

Ruth shook her head. "He doesn't have relatives, so . . .'

"I'll sort it," Josie said at once. "I've got some savings and I want to."

"Okay, I'll make sure it's you the morgue liaises with."

CHAPTER 31

"You take the car and go back to the station," Calladine told Rocco. "I'll go on foot, have a think, clear my head."

He left the Duggan and took the back road along the narrow lane that led towards the park and on into Leesdon centre. He strode on briskly for a good ten minutes, thinking of nothing in particular. The weak autumn sun peeked out from behind the clouds and felt warm on the back of his neck. It cheered him. Perhaps Ruth had something when she suggested a holiday. He heard someone call out to him. It was Kitty.

She leaned out of her car window. "I ring, you don't answer. I go round to your address but you're never there. Are you avoiding me?"

"Course not, it's just work," he said. "We've got a tricky case and it's taking all our resources and some. A policeman's lot isn't easy, you know."

"Hang on, I'll leave the car here and walk with you."

"Make sure you lock it," he said. "The Hobfield is just over there."

"Don't worry, it'll be fine." She hopped out of her car and took hold of his hand. "We'll walk through the park and get a coffee at that little hut. Then we'll sit on a bench and watch the world go by. When you feel better, you can return to work. I'll come back for my car later, then I'll go to my flat and cook dinner for you."

A generous offer. "You don't have to, really. I can get by, you know."

"I can imagine. I know what men living alone are like." She rolled her eyes.

Calladine didn't argue. He liked Kitty. Having a meal with her later would be no hardship at all.

Leesdon park was busy. School was over for the day and the kids were enjoying the pleasant weather while it lasted. Calladine sat down on a bench while Kitty went to get the drinks.

"I've got some brandy in my bag." She winked. "Fancy a drop in your coffee?"

He nodded and smiled. "But not a word. I'm still on duty."

She snuggled up close. "D'you have to go back? Wouldn't you rather come back with me, put your feet up?"

"I wish I could, but I've got too much to do. I'll see you later though, about 8 p.m.?"

"I suppose that's what I get for dating a detective. Tell me about your case," she asked. "What's making it so difficult?"

"A murdered woman, beaten to death, two lads shot in the head. Very different methods used, but we've found some forensic evidence to link them. Trouble is, I can't for the life of me understand it."

She smiled at him. "What a fascinating world you live in. What sort of forensic evidence?"

Calladine shook his head. "I can't discuss it. It's not public knowledge yet, hasn't been released to anyone outside the team."

Kitty pulled a face. "If you let me in, I might be able to help."

But Calladine wasn't listening. He was watching the steady stream of walkers entering and leaving the park via the gate that led on to the canal towpath. It was a well-trodden route — towpath, park and across the spare ground to the Hobfield. From the towpath you could walk all over Leesworth and up on to the hillside with no need to go near a road or a CCTV camera.

Kitty nudged him. "It's not good for you to be so preoccupied."

"I should go," he said. "I need to get some work done if I'm seeing you later."

"Okay, but try and shake the mood before tonight."

* * *

While Calladine was sitting on a park bench with Kitty, Greco and Ruth were in his office, deep in conversation. They were still talking when Calladine returned.

"Rocco back?" he asked Alice.

"No, he rang in, he's gone along the towpath with Julian's team," she said. "I've had a bit of luck," She handed him a sheet of paper. "Sarah Hammond, the third girl with Millie and Jade. I've found her."

"Great stuff," Calladine said. "Where's she living?"

"Well, she's not on the Hobfield any longer, far from it, and she's no longer a Hammond. She's called Sarah Cromwell, and lives in one of those new detached jobs in Hopecross, near Eve's place."

"So she's Eve's neighbour. That's a good place to start, chances are she knows her," he smiled. "It's a fairly close-knit community up there — money sticks together. And my mother knows all the gossip."

Eve Buckley was Tom Calladine's birth mother, though she hadn't raised him. That job had fallen to Freda, his father Frank Calladine's wife, and in Calladine's opinion, she'd made a good job of it and he wouldn't have wanted it any other way.

"Has Ruth told you what she and Greco found out?"

"Not really, just that they still don't know where Lazarov is. He's not with his girlfriend in Fallowfield and no one's seen him."

It was time to call it a day. One last visit and then he'd go home. "Tell anyone who asks that I'm on the trail of Sarah Hammond and I'll see them tomorrow."

CHAPTER 32

Eve Buckley ushered Calladine into her sitting room. "How come I only see you when it has something to do with work?"

Calladine kissed her cheek. "You know how it is, never lets up."

"Want to stay for some food?"

"I've made arrangements," he said. "But I will come for a proper visit once this case is sorted — me, Zoe and the infant."

"Little Maisie. I'm not sure what I think of that name, but I suppose it's not my place."

"Mine neither," he said. "It's Zoe's child and she can do as she sees fit. I don't even know if she's told Julian."

"You said on the phone that you wanted to know about the young woman up the road, Sarah Cromwell."

"I'm going to pay her a visit shortly and wondered what you knew about her. Her maiden name was Hammond, and when she was a kid she lived on the Hobfield. It's odd. Alice checked the records and couldn't find a Sarah Hammond or Cromwell in the marriage register."

"She's a cagey one. I was told that she changed her name. She's from a bad family on the Hobfield and can't bear to be reminded of it. She left the area in her teens. She's on the snooty side these days and trying very hard to put her past behind her."

"Any reason for the name change? Were her family villains?"

"Not really, it's just the Hobfield, Tom, simple as that. For a while she and Jack, her husband, lived in London but then his job brought him back here. Sarah wasn't at all happy about it at first."

"He's local too?" Calladine asked.

"Yes, but not from the Hobfield. His family lived in Lowermill."

"So, what's she hiding? What should I know about?"

Eve looked at him as if she knew something. "Well, rumour has it that she was involved with a bad bunch in her youth — drug dealers and the like — although she was very young at the time, still at school."

"D'you recall the Reed case?" he asked.

"The bones found up at Gorse House? Yes, of course I do. I knew Agnes Reed — well as much as anyone could know her. She was a strange one, that granddaughter of hers too. There was an incident, after which neither of them was ever seen again. Agnes had the stroke, of course, but I've no idea what became of the girl." She stared at her son accusingly. "I always wondered why you lot never bothered to investigate. She might have been a bit weird, but Millie was young, she went missing and no one gave her a second thought."

"It wasn't quite like that. We were led to believe she was staying with some relative. We still don't know what really happened," he said.

"I doubt Sarah will tell you even if she remembers — too protective of her reputation. She wouldn't want to become the subject of village gossip."

A problem he'd deal with when he met her. "What were they like, the Reeds?"

"Odd. Insular, the girl particularly. She had a hellish temper — I do remember that. She lost it once on the bus coming back from Oldston and went berserk. The pair were asked to get off. It was such a shame . . . she was a clever girl. Pretty, too, in spite of that mole on her cheek."

Calladine got to his feet. The day was fast disappearing, and he had a lot to do. "Thanks, that's been helpful."

She smiled. "I'll ring you to make arrangements for a proper meal. And I won't tolerate any excuses. Got that?"

* * *

He drove a little further up the hill to the Cromwell house. It was large — the entrance was protected by a heavy metal gate and the garden surrounded by trees. Calladine parked in the lane and walked round to a side gate. He could see a woman in the garden.

"Mrs Cromwell?" he called out.

She looked at him and frowned. "Who are you?"

"DI Calladine, Leesdon police." He showed her his warrant card. "If you've got a few minutes, I'd like a chat."

She came and unlocked the gate for him. "I can't see what I can possibly help you with," she said.

"It's not a recent matter," he said. "It's about what happened up at Gorse House that day."

"What day? What are you talking about?"

"The incident with Millie Reed and Jade O'Brien."

"Oh that. It was years ago, but it was no big deal," she said. "Millie invited us back after school—"

"And was never seen again," he said.

She turned away. "I don't know anything about that. It was just an ordinary visit. Millie showed us round the place and then we left."

"That's not what happened at all, is it, Mrs Cromwell? You see, I remember speaking to you at the time. You were scared, and I know that Jade O'Brien got injured."

She looked at him and narrowed her eyes. "You're that young detective, aren't you, the one who spoke to me."

"Yes. A rather green young detective, Mrs Cromwell."

"It was such a long time ago," she flustered. "You can't expect me to recall exactly what went on."

"You must have heard about the bones found up at the house?" he said.

"Yes, but they could belong to anyone."

"We don't think so," he said. "Currently the clever money is on them being Millie Reed's. There was a murder in Leesdon this week that has certain similarities, hence my interest in the Reed girl."

"Well, I can't help you. I have never harmed anyone, and anyway, it was all in the distant past. I can barely recall what happened."

She eyed him coldly. He wasn't going to get anything useful today. Calladine decided to leave it for now, but he'd speak to her again. His instinct told him Sarah Cromwell knew a lot more than she was saying, but he could only guess at her reasons for holding back.

CHAPTER 33

Calladine looked around. The sitting room was large with two comfy-looking sofas covered in cushions and a picture window looking out over the canal at the back of the old bank building. "You've made the place nice," he said.

Kitty shrugged. "It's not what I want though. As I told you, I'm after quaint. This place is okay, but the building has been modernized to within an inch of its life."

He settled on one of the sofas. "It'd do me. You work downstairs, too, no commute. The perfect set-up in my eyes."

"Well, not in mine. I want to go home and forget work at closing time. It might look modern on the surface, but the place is old, and it creaks. I hear the weirdest noises in the dead of night."

Calladine nodded. He knew a story about this building. No, perhaps he shouldn't tell it to her.

"What?" she asked, hands on her hips. "I saw that look. What doesn't Mr Policeman want to tell me?"

"Are you sure you want to know?" he said.

"I most certainly do. Now, give."

"I told you this used to be the village bank. Right next door is the museum. Well, back in the early 1950s the bank was raided, and a young copper was shot dead. The robbers knocked a hole in an adjoining wall. They got into the strong-room and tripped the alarm. The copper who was patrolling the street responded and got a bullet in the chest for his trouble."

"No one told me that," she exclaimed. "Did they get much money?"

Calladine shook his head. "No, they were stopped as they tried to leave. All I'm saying is that this building and the one next door have history and not all of it is good." He looked around and nodded. "I've always thought this place had an atmosphere, but you've changed that, given it a new lease of life."

She changed the subject. "Time to think about food. What d'you fancy eating? I'll have it sent up — steak, chips, some salad on the side?"

Calladine gave her a beaming smile. "Steak and chips will be fine. You can forget the salad."

"I'll go downstairs and organize it. There's a bottle of red there, would you open it?"

Kitty disappeared. Calladine dealt with the wine, poured himself a glass and idly looked at the photos on the sideboard. One showed a girl of about thirteen with blonde hair, wearing what looked like a Leesdon High uniform. It didn't register straight away — a measure of how tired he was. He returned to the comfort of the sofa, closed his eyes and took a sip of the wine. He was warm and relaxed for the first time in a while. He might have drifted off to sleep but the sound of his mobile startled him back into reality and drove away all thoughts of that photo.

He fished it out of his pocket, it was Rocco.

"We've brought a lad in, sir. I had a scout down the towpath with the forensic boys this afternoon and found this chancer selling dope to the kids."

"Is he one of Johnno's lot?" Calladine asked.

"No, he reckons he's working for the new firm. That's why I rang. Greco plans to interview him but I thought you should know."

The Lazarov part of this investigation wasn't down to him, but Rocco had been right to tell him.

"Has he said anything?" Calladine said.

"No. Reckons it's more than his life's worth," Rocco said.

"Is Ruth there?" Calladine asked.

"Yes. Shall I get her to ring you when they're done?"

"Yes. In the meantime, I want another word with Johnno Higgs." So much for the relaxing evening. "I've got to go, Kitty," he told her as soon as she returned.

"No, Tom. What about the food? Our evening together?"

"Sorry, but there'll be other times. I really do have to go."

* * *

Back in his car, Calladine rang Higgs. "I need a word. Where are you?"

"I'm staying with a mate — ground floor, Heron House. I'll look out for you."

Higgs had to know more than he'd told him. The man was scared — Calladine understood that. He was scared himself. He knew of old what Lazarov was capable of.

It took only minutes to reach the Hobfield. Johnno Higgs was waiting in the shadows outside the tower block. "Where are you living now?" Calladine asked.

"Moved into an empty one on the ground floor, just down the corridor there. As long as no one notices, I'll be sound."

"We've brought in a young lad caught dealing on the towpath. Who is he?" Calladine asked.

"How the hell should I know?" Higgs exclaimed. "It's nowt to do with me. I'm well out of the loop these days."

Calladine was wondering whether to believe him or not when he heard an owl hoot high up on the tower roof. Unusual and unexpected for a noisy estate allegedly awash with drugs. He looked around — the place was like the grave. There was no one about, no noise, no blaring music and certainly no kids on bikes delivering dope for the dealers. Something wasn't right.

"It's not usually like this. What's going on?"

"All quiet like, yeah. Has been for a while," Higgs said. "No good asking me why. I don't have a clue."

"So where does the dealing go on?" Calladine asked.

"I've told you — I don't know owt about it. I only know there's supposed to be someone new and he's a hard nut. Perhaps he's trying his luck in a more upmarket part of town. Well, good luck to him, that's what I say."

Calladine heaved a sigh. Perhaps Higgs was right. For as long as he could remember, the Hobfield had been the place to buy drugs in Leesdon. But wherever Lazarov was operating, it wasn't around here.

CHAPTER 34

His night ruined, all Calladine wanted to do was go home, call it a day. But there was a young lad at the station he needed to speak to.

Ruth met him at the station entrance. "This one's ours," she said at once.

"It's late. Have you managed to sort a sitter for Harry?" he said.

"Yes, Jake's round at mine. He knows my hours aren't regular and to expect his life to be disrupted occasionally. Serves him right."

"Have you spoken to the lad Rocco brought in yet?" Calladine asked.

"No, he's being processed. But there's no doubt he has been dealing. His pockets were full of little bags of cocaine."

"On his own, was he?" Calladine asked.

"Yes, but there's bound to be others. He'll tell us soon enough. Looks scared stiff to be honest," she said.

"Mind if I sit in?" he asked.

"I don't, but I don't know about Greco."

"I'll have a word." Calladine strode up the corridor to Greco's office. His case or not, he needed to test a theory.

"We can manage, you know," Greco said.

The DCI's face was expressionless, so Calladine couldn't tell if he was annoyed at his interference or not. "I'd like to ask the lad a couple of questions. The two cases do overlap where the forensics are concerned," he said.

"Okay, but don't upset him. He could be a direct route to Lazarov. Just what we need right now," Greco said.

Calladine nodded, but he doubted the lad knew anything about Lazarov. Something wasn't right and he was wondering just how much any of this was down to the Bulgarian villain.

Back in the incident room, Ruth handed him a file. "Arran Hughes, lives on the Hobfield, so he knows the estate well enough, and who his customers are."

Calladine skimmed through the notes. "He's been in bother before."

"A couple of stints in young offenders, both times dealing was involved, but he was always hanging on the coat-tails of someone older. Whether it's the same this time, he's not saying."

"Anyone with him when he was picked up?" Calladine asked.

"No. Arran reckons he was on his way back to the estate to check in with his boss."

"Has he said who that is?"

"No."

Rocco stuck his head around the office door. "We're on," he said.

"You don't have to be here," Ruth said again. "I'm sure you've got better things to do."

"I had. I was about to enjoy a pleasant supper with Kitty when Rocco rang."

"So, why sacrifice your evening for something we can deal with?" she said.

"I had a quick word with Johnno Higgs and realized this is more important," he said.

"Can't bear to be left out, Calladine, that's your problem."

The two of them made their way to the interview room. Greco and Rocco were already there, along with Arran Hughes and the duty solicitor. The lad was pale and looked as nervous as hell. He might have been in trouble with the police before, but he was no hard man.

"You were apprehended on the canal towpath, Arran," Greco began. "An amount of what we believe to be cocaine was found on your person. Tell me where you got it from."

The lad looked around at the others and then settled his gaze on Calladine. "It's not mine," he said.

"Yes it is, Arran. You were caught red-handed," Calladine said. "So why don't you save us all a lot of bother and tell us who you're working for."

The lad looked away. "Speak to you lot and I'll be a dead man."

"The coke, lad, who're you selling it for?" Calladine raised his voice. They'd be here all night at this rate.

"No one gave it me. I found it."

"Don't give me that rubbish," Calladine said. "If you don't start talking, you'll find yourself banged up for a long time."

"No!" squealed Arran. "You're supposed to release me, give me a warning and let me go."

Calladine shook his head. "Who told you that? You know it doesn't work like that. You've been in trouble before, Arran. You were brought in only three months ago with a large amount of cannabis on you. You obviously haven't learned your lesson, so the magistrates will take a dim view and sentence you accordingly."

Arran sounded close to tears. "I was paid to take the stuff and try to sell it. I didn't want to."

"Who paid you and supplied the goods?" Calladine asked.

"I was told where to pick up the stuff — a phone call, we never met. Then I had to go round the estate and get rid of it."

"Giving the stuff away, were you?" Calladine asked.

"No one was buying, and I got nervous. I had a lot of dope on me and the Hobfield isn't my patch."

"Were you working alone, Arran?" Ruth asked.

The lad nodded.

"Just tell us who you're working for, Arran," Calladine said.

"Like I said, this man rang me, told me where to find the coke. He said I should sell it and keep the proceeds. He said there'd be more work. It sounded like a good deal to me. I don't know his name and when I tried to ring him back, the number was discontinued."

"Can I have a word?" Greco asked Calladine. They went out into the corridor.

"He's guilty, there's no doubt about that. Brought in with the drugs on him, so we'll charge him and save ourselves a wasted night," Greco said. "When we go back in, ask him whatever it is you want to know and let's all go home."

"He was set up," Calladine said. "Whoever left the drugs for him used a burner phone. This is for our benefit, Stephen. We're supposed to link Arran Hughes to the new boss on the Hobfield. But that doesn't work for me. There's something wrong and I can't work out what it is. I was on the Hobfield tonight, wanted a word with Higgs. There's nothing happening — no dealing, no kids and no one looking to buy. I don't know why, but someone is trying very hard to make it appear that we've got a new drugs baron in the area, but I don't see the evidence. So far, all we've got is a few hundred pounds' worth of coke and one frightened lad."

"Lazarov?"

"Still not sure, but I intend to find out."

"You get off, I'll charge the lad and call it a day."

CHAPTER 35

Day Five

"I got the feeling that Greco wasn't best pleased last night. What did you say to him?" Ruth asked. "You both buggered off into the corridor, you disappeared, and he came back into the room in a right mood."

Ignoring her question, Calladine merely said, "Did the lad say anything else?"

"No, he kept on saying he just picked the stuff up and insists he hasn't a clue who is behind it. He's in front of the magistrate this morning and will probably get bail."

"He could be telling the truth," Calladine said.

"What? What's got into you? Course he's not. Arran Hughes is working for Lazarov, has to be," she said.

"We'll see."

"What're you up to this morning?" Ruth asked.

"I want another word with Sarah Cromwell," he said.

"You only saw her yesterday."

"She was cagey, holding back," Calladine said. "We'll push her a bit, see how she responds."

"We? I'm supposed to be working with Greco, not you. Have you cleared it with him?"

He hadn't. Calladine couldn't get used to not having Ruth with him. Besides, he hoped a female officer might get more out of Mrs Cromwell, and she might even remember Ruth from school. "I'll see if Greco'll take Rocco this morning. Can't see how he can refuse. Rocco brought Hughes in and knows the drug haunts on the Hobfield. Greco, being the man he is, will want to make absolutely sure that Hughes wasn't spinning us a yarn."

Ruth nodded. "Sarah was pally with Jade and her gang when we were young. I only vaguely recollect her, she was the quiet one, more of a tag-a-long than a proper gang member. She was a lot easier to get on with than the others. I think she actually had a conscience."

"She's the one who looked shifty when I spoke to them twenty-odd years ago. She wanted to say something but was afraid of what Jade would do, I reckon," he said.

Ruth raised an eyebrow. "Weren't we all back then."

"When we're done with her, I'd like to take a look at Gorse House."

"What for? There's nothing there," Ruth said.

"Perhaps not but just indulge me. It's central to the case and I haven't been up there in all these years. Anyway, according to Long's file there are still a couple of buildings standing, an old workshop and a summer house. I'll have that word with Greco, and we'll get off."

* * *

Once Calladine explained how Ruth might help prise information out of Sarah Cromwell, Greco was fine with the swap.

"What do you think she isn't telling you, then?" Ruth asked.

"The truth," he said. "She knows what happened that day, and for reasons I don't understand, she's still too scared to say anything."

"Her reasons are simple — Jade."

"Not after all this time, surely?" Calladine said. "Jade can't hurt her now. No, Ruth, there has to be something else.

I think that under the influence of Jade, those girls deliberately hurt Millie Reed. That's what she's afraid will come out. And if I'm right, that makes her an accessory to murder."

"But you saw Millie coming home from school. You said as much," Ruth said.

Ruth was right. When he'd seen the Reed girl, it had been from a distance but she appeared to be fine. "There's always the theory that those girls went back up there, and Jade got her revenge."

"I don't see it," she said. "Jade had a head injury. Within a couple of days she was in a coma in hospital."

It was a mystery, but there had to be an explanation. Calladine was certain that whatever happened to Millie Reed that day was central to this current case.

Sarah Cromwell wasn't pleased to see them. She let them into the house and showed them into a small room overlooking the back garden. "My husband is upstairs working. I'd rather he didn't know too much about this."

"Why? Afraid of what he might find out?" Calladine said.

She glared at him. "Jack knows very little about my past. He doesn't even know that I grew up on the Hobfield." She sniffed. "And given how he feels about that place, I'd prefer it to stay that way."

"Where you were raised is of no interest to us, Mrs Cromwell. All I want is the truth about what happened the day Jade was injured. Then we'll happily leave you in peace."

She looked at Ruth and her eyes widened. "I know you. From school. You were a few years behind us."

"Yes, and I remember you and the girls you hung out with."

"I bet you do. We terrorized the lot of you. We practically ran that school. Had Jade not been attacked, perhaps in time she'd have ruled the entire estate." She hung her head. "I'm sorry for what we did back then, for how we were. If anything we did or said upset you personally, then I can only apologize.

"I did my best to keep out of your way," Ruth said. "I kept my head down, we all did."

Sarah sighed. "Shame Millie didn't think the same."

"What happened, Sarah? How was Jade injured?" Calladine asked. "We know Millie Reed disappeared, but we have no idea why. Perhaps you can tell us about that, too."

"This is your chance to come clean, Sarah, to put the record straight," Ruth urged.

Sarah looked into the distance. "I admit I lied to you back then. We did go up to Millie's house that day and Jade was itching for a fight. We'd gone into the workshop outside to look for gear Jade could give Johnno to sell. Jade teased Millie all the time, and that day was no different. I think she was jealous of the girl, of how pretty she was and the fact that she lived in a big house and had nice things. But Jade didn't know when to stop. She picked up a Stanley knife and lunged at her, threatened to cut off the mole on her face. She must have hurt her because there was a lot of blood and Millie looked shocked. If that wasn't enough, Jade snatched a locket Millie wore around her neck. It looked expensive — gold, with Millie's initials on it."

Calladine got out his mobile and found the photo of the image drawn in blood. He showed it to Sarah. "Did the locket look anything like this?"

"That's a crude representation, but yes," Sarah said.

"What happened next?"

"Suddenly, everything changed. Millie lost it, and went for Jade with a hammer. Jade fell down and then Millie hit Kaz." Sarah shook her head. "I didn't hang around. I ran for my life — the girl had gone berserk. I didn't know how badly Jade or Kaz was hurt, I just wanted to get out of there in one piece." She looked at their faces as if trying to read what they were thinking. "That's the truth. Millie invited us back after school and we saw it as an opportunity to have a laugh. If I could go back and change events, I would, but what's done is done."

"What happened to the locket?" Calladine asked.

"Jade kept it, treated it as some sort of trophy, kept showing it off on the way home. The picture you've just shown me — it looks like it was drawn in blood. Where did you find it?"

"I can't tell you, Sarah," Calladine said. "I'll ask you to keep that particular piece of information to yourself — and the whole thing about the locket."

"We know Jade ended up in hospital and the injury affected her for life," Ruth said. "What happened to the other girl, Kaz?"

"That same day, Jade's mum overdosed and was hospitalized. I went with Jade to see her. Kaz told us she and her mum had had a bust up, and her mum had done one. The bailiffs were about to turf them out of the flat anyway. Kaz's mum went to live with a friend in Oldston. I think Kaz went to stay with someone near Whitby."

"Are you sure about that?" Calladine said.

"Well, no, but that's what I was told."

"She never got in touch after that?" Calladine asked.

"No. We never heard from her or her mum again."

"What is Kaz's full name?" Calladine asked.

"Karen Thornton."

Calladine noted the name down. "How was Jade when you went with her to see her mum?"

"Weird. She kept falling asleep and complaining her head hurt. We had to practically carry her home between us. It was while we were there that she passed out for the first time."

"You do remember me, don't you?" Calladine said. "You said you did when we spoke before. I talked to you on the afternoon of the incident, and when I visited the hospital to speak to Jade."

"I'm not sure now. I think so, because after the fight, I went home and stayed in my room. I do remember thinking that Millie's granny was bound to complain, and then you'd come back and arrest us all."

"But you saw Jade later that day."

"She asked me to go to the hospital with her to see her mother. I only stayed an hour. Becca was fast asleep and like I said, Jade kept passing out. I just presumed she'd had some of what her mother had taken."

Ruth smiled at her. "Thanks, Sarah, for being so honest with us."

"Why were you so afraid to speak to me before?" Calladine asked.

"Because I didn't want to get involved. It was a long time ago, and I'm a different person now with a different life. I didn't want something from that time pinning on me. It's as simple as that."

What she'd told them explained a lot. Next on the list to speak to was Karen Thornton — if they could find her. "Do you have a photo of the three of you taken around that time?" he asked.

Sarah went into the sitting room and returned with an album. "This is the netball team. Me, Jade, Kaz — and that girl there is Millie." She pointed.

"May I take this? I'll bring it back when the case is over."

He and Ruth left, taking the photo with them. Asking Ruth to drive, Calladine sat in the passenger seat staring at the photo, deep in thought. It was the figure of Millie Reed that intrigued him. It wasn't particularly clear, but it reminded him of another photo he'd seen recently. The one in Kitty's flat.

CHAPTER 36

Gorse House had stood on the hillside above Leesdon for nearly 200 years, but there was nothing left of it now except for a couple of ramshackle outbuildings. Back in the Reeds' time the house had been surrounded by trees. Today, those same trees were taller, and saplings encroached on the space the house had once occupied. Soon, there'd be nothing to show that there'd ever been a house there at all.

The house was approached by a narrow road to one side and a footpath over the hill on the other. "I drove as far as here," Calladine said suddenly, breaking his silence. "On the road we've just come along. I spoke to the granny and as I was leaving, I saw the girl coming along the path opposite."

"The road comes up here from Leesdon, that path goes down to Lowermill. Millie was supposedly returning home from school," Ruth reminded him. "Well, she was walking home from the wrong direction. Which bears out what Sarah said about the fight. Millie wasn't coming back from school; she'd been here the whole time. It was a ruse cooked up by her and her granny to make you think she hadn't been around."

"You're suggesting that a police visit was anticipated, so the old woman was making it look as if nothing had happened, and that the girls were lying?" Calladine said.

"Yes. Sarah, Johnno and even Jade, in her more lucid moments, all agree that the girls were here with Millie after school. They can't all have been lying. Didn't you notice blood on her face? Jade had cut her mole. It'd have bled a lot."

Calladine shook his head. "I wasn't close enough. If I'd waited, spoken to her, things might have been different." Ruth was right. So why would Agnes Reed lie? Why not come clean and tell him that her granddaughter had been attacked? It could only be because she was hiding something, or to protect Millie.

"Wouldn't fancy living up here when it snows." Ruth got out of the car. "There's a weird atmosphere, too. Listen to the way the wind rustles through the trees, like they're whispering secrets to one another."

He chuckled. "Very fanciful, Sergeant Bayliss."

"There is an eeriness about the place though. Don't you think so?"

"I always did. When I came up on that day, I stood right over there where those flagstones are. Back then, they were right outside the back door. The old woman stood on the doorstep to talk to me, but I never went inside."

Ruth shuddered. "What did it look like, the house?"

"Stone-built, three storeys high, standing grey and gaunt against the skyline," he said. "There was smoke coming out of the chimney, and I remember thinking it odd because it was a warm day."

"There's little sign of the house now," Ruth said, looking around. "A few stones, those flags and some depressions in the ground."

"You know, there's no mention of the locket in any of the reports, either from the time of the incident or when the bones were found. But Becca's killer must have known about it. Narrows the field a little, don't you think?"

She looked at him. "All the way down to Jade."

But Calladine had stopped listening. He was walking round what he guessed to be the perimeter of the building. "Big place. Must have cost a bit to maintain."

"Shame no one kept it up," Ruth said.

"No one left interested enough."

"Which is why the house had to be torn down," Ruth said. "Mind you, I can't imagine anyone wanting to buy it. It is strange up here. I wouldn't want to wander around after dark. It's the sort of place you'd have to make sure you locked up tight every night."

He grinned. "Given the way the world is, I would hope you do that wherever you are." He pointed. "Over there. That must be the workshop, and that other wooden structure the summer house."

"The workshop is in reasonable nick, but the other building is a shambles."

Calladine went over to the crumbling summer house. The roof was caved in and the inside full of leaves from the surrounding trees. It was empty.

Ruth was trying the door of the workshop. "It's locked," she called back. She grabbed hold of the padlock and shook it. "Strange. This padlock is fairly new."

Calladine joined her. "All the more reason to get inside. There's a wrench in the boot of the car, go and fetch it, would you?"

"Breaking and entering, Mr Calladine. Goodness. You can get sent down for that."

The wrench made short work of the lock. The workshop was dark and felt damp. Calladine pointed to the ceiling. "Slate missing."

"There's an old bench here," Ruth said. She bent down, there was something underneath it. "Camping equipment," she said. "Someone's been dossing down in here."

"What's that over there?" Calladine said.

In the farthest corner of the room, almost hidden in the shadows, was a bulky rectangular shape covered in tarpaulin. Calladine walked across and pulled it off to reveal a battered old chest freezer.

"Not plugged in and old as the hills," Ruth said. "Probably belonged to the Reeds. Don't know why anyone would keep it, thing's practically rusted away."

"There's no electricity so pointless plugging it in. I'm more interested in why it's been padlocked, too."

Ruth handed him the wrench and stood back. Minutes later, the padlock clattered to the floor and Calladine lifted the heavy lid.

The smell hit them first. Both knew that smell only too well — the rancid stench of death. Inside the freezer, with his legs bent and twisted to fit, was the body of a man.

Ruth clamped her scarf over her nose. "He's not been here long but locked in like that the smell had nowhere to go. Poor bugger. Wonder what he did to deserve this."

Calladine was silent. He stared down at the remains. "I know this man, and so do you. That in there is what's left of Andrei Lazarov."

CHAPTER 37

Within the hour, the workshop at the Gorse House site was crowded with Natasha and Julian's people.

"Single gunshot between the eyes, same as the two lads," Natasha told the pair.

"How long has he been dead?" Calladine asked.

"From the look of him, at a rough guess I'd say a day, possibly two," she said.

"He rang me yesterday morning — in the early hours," Calladine said. "Wonder who he upset to end up here. I thought Lazarov was the one at the top of the tree. Seems I was wrong."

Ruth nudged him. "Greco's here."

Greco hurried over to where Calladine and Ruth stood. "What's going on, Tom? And why here of all places?"

That was puzzling Calladine too. It had to mean that the two cases — Becca and the shootings — were linked in some way. "I've no idea, Stephen," he said. He caught sight of Julian and went for a word.

"I've never actually met Lazarov," he told Julian. "I recognized him because I've seen a photo. Before we start concocting a load of wild theories, would you first make an official identification?"

"Of course, Tom," Julian said. "His prints and DNA are on record."

Greco approached them. "I've spoken to both Manchester and Huddersfield. They weren't much help. They went after Lazarov when he was living in Fallowfield and missed him. His lady friend told Ruth and me he'd disappeared a month ago."

"He was alive and well yesterday morning. He rang me, making the usual threats against me and my family."

"You should have told me that immediately," Greco said.

"Getting bloody used to it, aren't I?" Calladine went outside into the fresh air. He couldn't think straight in there, what with the chatter and forensic bods milling around. He needed to work out what on earth was going on — Becca O'Brien beaten to death, two lads shot in the same way as Lazarov, and all linked to Gorse House. Why? What was he missing here?

Ruth came out to join him. "What is this, Ruth? It's not drugs, I'm sure about that."

"Why not drugs? Isn't that what him in there was famous for?" she said.

"Him in there is dead," he said pointedly. "And that means we've got to go right back to the beginning. Lazarov was the only one in the frame, there's no one else, Ruth."

"We don't suspect him of killing Becca, that one's personal. But he could still be responsible for shooting those two lads."

She was right. "We were so certain Lazarov was the new threat, the one with big ambitions for dealing in the area. It looks as if that might be right, but someone didn't like his plans."

"Johnno?" Ruth said. "He could have got fed up of being sidelined, decided to do something about it."

"Not his style, Ruth."

"Could it be down to one of his people then? They have a row, Lazarov is killed. We know how often the people behind the dealing fall out," she said.

"Do we though? I'm not sure there's any dealing going on at all. I was on the Hobfield last night and it was quiet — no one about, and certainly no one dealing."

"There wouldn't be, not with Lazarov dead," Ruth said. "This venture is in its infancy. Lazarov was still hiring recruits."

Calladine wandered off towards the perimeter of the house with a bewildered Ruth following him. "She was found down there." He pointed. "Dressed in her school uniform and curled up into a ball."

"Poor girl, she didn't deserve any of it. Back to the Lazarov thing — you reckon it's not drugs, but I still think it's a possibility," Ruth said. "It's the only thing that makes any sense. We should find out if any of Lazarov's people are still hanging around."

Calladine shook his head. "I'm still undecided."

Greco picked his way across the rough ground to join them. "Lazarov won't have come to the area alone," he said, echoing Ruth's words. "Whoever was here with him, they need rounding up and bringing in."

Calladine didn't respond. Before he committed himself to anything, he had to talk to Johnno Higgs again. He stood staring into the trees, deep in thought. There were the usual woodland varieties but there were others too, he spotted them beyond a couple of oaks. Near to where the back of the house must have stood, he saw a group of alder buckthorn trees dripping berries, which were scattered on the ground beneath them. He pointed. "Ruth! Look. We've found our trees."

"Makes sense, given we know Lazarov is here. Adds weight to the theory that he killed Becca and the lads."

A good theory and they now had some evidence to back it up, but Calladine couldn't work out why he should kill Becca. The killings were different, but were the motives? "I'm going back to town," he said and marched off to his car, Ruth trailing in his wake.

"Want to share what's going on in your brain?" she said. "I know this is a struggle and it hasn't turned out as we thought, but we just have to think again."

"Think what, Ruth? I was led to believe that the new order in Leesdon was run by Lazarov. I got phone calls. My family was threatened. Now I find the man dead. That makes me wonder who was pulling Lazarov's strings."

"Well at least you can bring Zoe and the babe back from the safe house now, since Lazarov is no longer a threat."

He sat quietly behind the wheel of his car. "But someone else might be." He glanced at her. "I've been manipulated. This entire drugs thing is a set-up."

"Are you sure? Is this 'set-up' as you call it deliberate and not just someone trying to pin the venture on Lazarov to keep us in the dark about who's really behind the drugs takeover?"

"Who knows? I'm racking my brain. Right now, I've no clue what's going on. I'm hoping Julian finds some forensics that will help us. Meanwhile, I want another chat with Johnno."

"Want me to drive?" Ruth offered. "You seem a bit overwrought. I drive, then you can phone Higgs, make sure he's in and we'll go and see him."

"Yes, okay." Ruth got out and he slid across. "I need a bloody rest," he said. "When this is over, I'm going to take that holiday you spoke about."

"Great idea. Shame I don't have any time owing or I'd come with you."

CHAPTER 38

Johnno Higgs agreed to meet them at the same place as before, in front of Heron House on the Hobfield. He was nervous, his gaze constantly darting around.

"Lazarov is dead," Calladine told him.

"The foreign-sounding bloke?" Higgs smiled. "That means we can breathe easy."

Calladine, hands in his overcoat pockets, sighed. If it was only that simple. "I'm not so sure. The fact that he's dead means the man I had in mind for the dealing — your foreign bloke — isn't in charge after all. It also means that someone deliberately led me to believe he was. We've been looking for the wrong man. That's why we need your help, Johnno."

"I don't know owt, Mr Calladine, only what I've already told you."

Calladine nodded towards the hills. "Have you ever gone up there to have a look at what's left of Gorse House?"

"No. I never went up there before, so why would I now?"

"D'you know anyone who has? Jade, Becca, anyone?"

Higgs shook his head. "People tend to avoid the place. They reckon it's haunted. That girl — you know, Millie."

"That's nonsense," Calladine said firmly. "Tell me about the drug dealing. Who's running things and how much of it is going on."

Higgs raised his hands. "Uh-uh. I do that and I'm in big trouble."

"Why? Someone threatened you?"

"No, but I talk and the only person who gets hauled in is me," Higgs said.

Calladine shook his head. "Not this time, Johnno. Tell me everything you know and this conversation never happened."

"You won't charge me?" Higgs said.

Calladine felt Ruth nudge him — she didn't like this, but right now he didn't care. This case needed sorting and there were things they had to know. "No, Johnno, you can say what you want to us and it'll be totally off the record. Let's pretend, just for tonight, that I'm not a policeman."

Higgs lit a cigarette. He took several deep drags and, looking at Calladine long and hard, began to speak. "The foreign man — he was throwing his weight around, forcing the lads on the estate to work for him. I had to keep my head down. He was dangerous, carried a gun and, as you know, was happy to use it. I have a regular supplier who drops stuff off and I have a round of customers I see to. I don't do much dealing, just enough to keep me in food and fags, you know how it is. The foreigner threatened me, said all that had to stop and that I was working for him now."

"How did you react?" Calladine asked.

"How d'you think? I dropped out of sight for a while. That's why I was so worried about Becca the night she died. I knew that if I couldn't sort her out, she'd get in touch with the new crew."

"You said the stuff being touted around was cheap, and whoever was responsible had plenty of muscle to call on."

"That's right, Mr Calladine. I never actually saw anything for myself, but I asked around. My usual customers had seen

163

some rough stuff and one bloke got beat up for refusing to buy from them. You say he's dead. That figures. Since yesterday, it's all gone quiet and right now the estate is trouble-free. That's how I like to operate."

Calladine nodded. "Thanks, Johnno, that's been a great help."

They stood and watched him slope off into the tower block.

"D'you believe him?" Ruth asked. "Or was all that just Johnno Higgs covering his tracks?"

"He's got a good thing going — small-time, but he's always operated that way. He doesn't want any trouble. No, Lazarov started this and whoever he's working for decided to put a stop to it, effectively ending the impending drugs war. He's got some other motive for being here." He heaved a deep sigh. "What we have to do now is work out what it is."

"Want to go back to the station and eat?" Ruth asked.

"You go. Take the car, I need a walk, give myself a chance to think. But you can do one thing. Ask Alice to have a go at finding the third girl, Karen Thornton."

* * *

Calladine headed back along the canal towpath, through the park and out on to the road that ran through Leesdon centre. The place was busy. He waved at a couple of people he knew, including an elderly woman who'd been a friend of Freda's.

"I'm told you've got a new grandchild," she called out. "Congratulations. Freda would be proud."

Calladine smiled and nodded. She was right there.

"Who'd have thought it, you a grandad." The voice came from behind him. "I envy you, Tom. I'll never have grand-children now."

He swung round and came face to face with Marilyn Fallon. "What are you doing here?" He was surprised to find her wandering around the town free as a bird. "I thought Debra Weller would drop you off, or at least contact me first."

"I'm out on parole, remember? You were told. And Debra did drop me off, but you weren't in. Debra got an urgent call and had to take off. I was on my way to the station to find you."

Marilyn looked well, slimmer than he remembered. He noted her smart jacket and the fact that she was wearing make-up. "I'm just on my way home for a spot of lunch and to take Sam for a walk."

"He barked at me." She sounded put out. "I tapped on the window and he responded with a nasty growl. I swear he doesn't remember who I am."

"He will. He's a good lad is Sam. And dogs don't forget."

They turned into Calladine's street of identical stone-built terraced houses.

"Don't you ever fancy a change?" Marilyn asked, glancing at the small front garden. "You've got a good job, surely you can afford to live somewhere better?"

"I like it here, it suits me. Anyway, I was born on this street, six doors up. Ray too. Francis, Freda's sister and Ray's mother, stayed with Freda while she was pregnant with Ray. She gave birth here and then went to live with that loser of a man she took up with."

"I don't know much about Ray's background, he never told me. Perhaps you could fill me in sometime."

The last thing Calladine wanted to do was spend hours talking about Ray Fallon. As far as he was concerned, Ray was better off consigned to history and never mentioned again.

"You want to know about family history, get yourself down to the library," he told her. "My head's too full of other stuff."

CHAPTER 39

Calladine sat in front of the fire with a cup of tea in his hand and Sam at his feet. The dog had taken no notice of Marilyn at all. She'd patted his head, tickled him behind his ears, but he remained indifferent. Miffed at her reception, she'd disappeared upstairs to sort out her stuff.

Calladine needed a rest, some space to go over the complexities and mysteries of this case in his head. Lazarov had been up to his old tricks and had been shot dead for his trouble, but by who? Someone who wasn't keen on starting a new drugs war, that's who. If he was right, what were they after? His reverie was interrupted by the reappearance of Marilyn.

"The wallpaper in that back bedroom is the same as when I was last here. You haven't touched the place in years, Tom."

"I like things as they are," he said. "I don't do change for its own sake."

"It's old-fashioned, and as for the furniture, well, very forties. Even the junk shop wouldn't give it houseroom."

"It came from Freda's. If it suited her then it suits me."

"I'm not surprised you never got married again," she said. "What woman would put up with your stuck-in-a-rut ways? No one I know, that's for sure."

That was a relief. There was no way he'd be interested in any friend of Marilyn's. He listened to her mutter to herself as she went out to the kitchen. He'd have to learn to switch her off or it'd drive him mad. Calladine gave Sam another pat, leaned back and closed his eyes.

If the case wasn't about dealing, then what was it about? What was important enough that the local police had to be kept so busy and tied up in knots that they didn't have time to draw breath or think straight? Someone who didn't want their plans interfering with.

"I'm going for a walk," Marilyn announced. She looked at the dog. "Sam? Want to come?"

The dog didn't so much as twitch. He wasn't interested. Calladine couldn't be more pleased. "No, he doesn't want to go. Leave him. You'll need a key. I might not be here when you get back." He tossed her one off the sideboard. "Get yourself some food, I'll sort my own."

"Are you always like this, Tom?" she asked.

"Like what?"

"Preoccupied. Boring. Falling asleep in the afternoon. When did that start? You're turning into an old man, Tom Calladine."

Calladine was heartily relieved when she finally walked out the door. It wasn't going to be easy, but if he kept out of her way, he might last out.

His mobile rang. It was Julian.

"I think we need a meeting to discuss findings so far. I have several things to report on and it would be easier to explain if you, Ruth and the others met me in the lab."

"When?" Calladine asked him.

"We are fast-tracking some of the samples collected from the workshop at Gorse House, and there are results from the O'Brien flat. Tomorrow after lunch will be fine."

"Okay. Will you ring Ruth and get her to tell the others?"

It was something at least. Julian was the best. If anyone could find them the evidence to break this case, it would be him. Calladine was about to leave the house when his phone rang again. This time it was Kitty.

"I've got serious withdrawal," she purred. "I want to see you, and soon. Our last date never happened, if you remember. We didn't even get a chance to eat. What about tonight?"

What with the case and Marilyn he wasn't really in the mood, but the food in that restaurant was top-notch. He liked Kitty, plus she was far better company than Marilyn. "Okay, I'll come to yours for 8 p.m.," he said.

"I'm looking forward to it, and don't be late."

It would be a welcome break from the harpy and her criticisms of his lifestyle. It wasn't late, still mid-afternoon. Calladine decided to return to the station and look through the reports and statements again.

He patted the dog. "Want to go see Ryan across the road? He'll take you for walkies." Calladine knew the lad would look after him — he liked Sam — and he'd pick him up at the end of the evening on his way back from Kitty's. Better all round if Sam was kept out of Marilyn's clutches.

CHAPTER 40

"I didn't expect you back," Ruth said. "Sorted your head out?"

"Not really, but I'll get there eventually. Anything come in?"

"Only the meeting with Julian tomorrow. He wants Greco there, too."

"Well, he is SIO on the Lazarov case. The remit might have changed — now he's looking for his killer instead of trying to bring him in — but there's still plenty of work to do."

He left Ruth and went into his office. On the desk were two stacks of paperwork — one connected with Millie Reed and the other the murder of Becca O'Brien.

He started on the Reed pile and went through the notes yet again. There was a photograph showing a blonde girl, pretty but with a prominent mole or birthmark on the upper half of her right cheek. He stared at it. She'd be the same age as she was in the photo Sarah Cromwell had shown them.

He went out into the main office. "Ruth. You knew Millie at school. What was she like?"

"Clever, pretty, and bullied by Jade and her mates."

"The birthmark on her face. Was she teased about that?" he asked.

"Yes, they made fun of her all time because of it. She was very aware of it and believed it spoiled her looks. But it wasn't a birthmark, more a sizeable mole. Personally, I thought it suited her — you know, like a beauty spot. But Jade and her gang used it to torment her. If she'd lived, Millie could have had it removed no problem."

"Sarah told us that Jade had a go at the mole with a Stanley knife." Ruth winced. "I didn't get close enough to her that day to see if she was injured or not, but she must have been, and there'd have been blood. Perhaps that's when some of it got on to her skirt."

"If she'd lived, there would have been a scar, too. How bad is anyone's guess, we don't know how deep the cut was," Ruth said.

"Eve said she had a hellish temper," Calladine said. "Did you ever see anything of that?"

Ruth looked puzzled. "No. I always thought her a sweet girl, older than me but young for her age if you know what I mean."

"You're sure? No sudden outbursts? Shows of violence?"

Ruth laughed. "What are you getting at? Even if the girl was all those things, what difference would it make now? She's long gone. It's not Millie Reed who's been going around Leesworth killing people."

But Calladine wasn't so sure. He said nothing. There were things he needed to check first. Something had niggled at the back of his mind ever since he'd seen the photo Sarah had shown them. He looked at Ruth. He couldn't say anything to her until he was absolutely sure. "You're right. It's me, I'm clutching at straws."

"There's not a lot going on here. Rocco is still up at Gorse House with Greco and Julian is busy with whatever his team have collected. Alice is working on the Karen Thornton thing, so why don't you go home, get an early night?"

He nodded. "I might just do that. I've looked through those reports so many times I know them off by heart. You make an early dart too — get off home and spend some time with that lad of yours."

"Are you letting Zoe come home?" she asked as he put his coat on.

"Not yet. Call me overcautious, but I believe the danger is still out there."

* * *

Calladine decided not to go home before going to Kitty's but to pay another visit to Eve, his mother. When she'd said Millie had a temper, he hadn't thought about it at the time, but now he was curious.

"Twice in one week, I am honoured," she said. "But it'll be work. I don't flatter myself that you'd trail up here for a catch-up. Come through, I'll get us a pot of tea and you can bore me to tears with your latest case."

He forced a laugh. "I'm not that bad, am I? It's just another run-of-the-mill murder — well murders actually — and the man we had down as the main suspect has turned up dead himself. How's that for a major setback?"

She looked at him, frowning. "Oh dear, you are down, aren't you? But you shouldn't be. You'll work it out, Tom, you usually do."

He flopped into one of her armchairs that had a view out into the back garden. It looked wild and windswept, all bare branches and no leaves left on the trees. "Millie Reed," he began. "Tell me about her."

Eve Buckley sat down opposite her son and shrugged. "Not a lot to tell really. A serious girl, small for her age, though I always thought she had hidden depths. You know the type, all meek and sweet on the surface but churning away underneath."

"You said she had a temper," he said.

"Indeed she did. I witnessed it myself and I saw the bruises on Agnes. Her arms were covered in them, her face too a couple of times. That can only have been down to Millie — there was only the two of them up at that house. She must have packed quite a punch for such a delicate-looking child."

"Did you know she was bullied at school?" Calladine said.

"I heard that and thought it odd. Maybe she was wicked to her granny but afraid to stand up to her peers. I was only on nodding terms with Agnes, but occasionally we'd stop to chat about the weather, and that's when I noticed the bruises. There was no husband, no one else at all, so the girl was her only companion. Agnes never complained though."

"Thanks. I'm not sure how it helps, but it gives me a rounder picture of the girl."

"Glad to help. Are you staying for tea?"

"I can't," he said. "I've got a date."

CHAPTER 41

Any other time, Calladine would have looked forward to dinner with Kitty, but not tonight. Tonight, he had to decide. Was she as she appeared to be, who she said she was? It was going to make for a difficult conversation.

He'd looked at the photo in her flat — the pretty young blonde girl in her school uniform. He'd also seen two of Millie Reed — one in the file at work and the one Sarah had shown him. It had taken all day for the penny to drop, but finally he realized that it could be the same girl in all three photos. If there was the remotest possibility that Kitty was in fact Millie Reed, then she was the prime suspect for Becca O'Brien's murder.

He'd discussed none of this with Ruth or the team. He wanted to make some headway before landing them with another problem. Like if not the Reed girl, then who did the bones buried up at Gorse House belong to? His money was on Karen Thornton. She'd been injured and hadn't been seen from that day to this.

He used the back entrance to the restaurant and took the stairs up to Kitty's flat. He wasn't looking forward to this evening. Either way, it would mean an end to their relationship. How could Kitty continue to trust him if within a week of meeting her he suspected her of being a fraud and a killer? If he was right, the outcome would be worse. What about the two lads and Lazarov? He knew the killings were linked. Whoever killed all three of them had been in the vicinity of those berries, which meant Gorse House.

"Mr Policeman," she said, kissing his cheek. "Will we get to spend time together tonight or will you cut and run as usual?"

"I'll do my best," he muttered. "Have you owt to drink?" He needed Dutch courage. If he was going to accuse this woman of murder, he'd like a couple of whiskies inside him first.

"Wine's in the kitchen, but more important, what d'you want to eat?"

"That steak and chips I missed out on will do nicely, and have you got anything stronger than wine?"

With a smile, she took a bottle of single malt from the shelf. "I'll go down and sort the food."

She was trying to please, and he hated himself for his suspicions. He doubted he'd be able to eat the food when it arrived. She disappeared downstairs, leaving him pacing up and down nervously. The photo was still there. He picked it up. It still looked like a Leesdon High uniform and Kitty still looked like Millie. It had to be faced, and it didn't augur well for the evening to come. His hand was even shaking, not like him. He had to remain cool.

"I went to see one of those houses along the canal this morning," she said on her return. "You weren't around, so Ronan came with me. He was his usual helpful self, pointed out a couple of things, so provided the sellers are happy to reduce the price, I might make an offer."

"See a lot of Ronan?" he asked, trying to sound casual.

"He only works next door, so, yes, I see him most days." She smiled. "But don't be jealous, he's got a woman. I saw them together just this afternoon, in fact. Very close they looked, too."

"Did you go to Leesdon High?" He cursed himself. He hadn't meant to blurt it out like that. It was an odd question and out of context. Kitty frowned, looking puzzled.

"The school uniform in the photo over there? Is that what you mean?" she asked. "It's not Leesdon High. I didn't live here as a child, I told you, Tom, I just visited the hills, but I suppose one school uniform is much the same as another. The usual navy skirt and blazer with a white shirt."

He took her hand and led her over to the lamp. There, in the light, he saw it. High on her right cheek there was the faintest trace of a scar. He felt sick. His instinct had been right. He ran a finger over it, gently. "Where did you get that?"

"An accident when I was a kid. Fell off my bike. Made a helluva mess at the time." She grimaced. "But the hospital were wonderful, did all they could so it wouldn't leave too much of a mark."

It sounded plausible and she had no problem relating the tale. There was no stumbling or awkwardness when she told him.

"Is it that important? Don't you want me if I'm scarred? Damaged goods?" she said, making light of it.

"It's not that." Calladine was too afraid to confront her with it. He couldn't do it, not now, to her, not just yet. He didn't want to believe what his reason was telling him must be the case. "Look, I'm sorry but I have to go. I'll make it up to you another time." He grabbed his overcoat and without a backward glance, fled down the stairs. Out on Lowermill High Street, he gasped for breath. Was this a panic attack? Was he ill? He had no idea, and right now he didn't care. He was just pleased to be out of there and away from Kitty.

"I thought you were staying for supper," someone said from behind him. "Kitty's talked about little else all day."

Calladine looked round. It was the man from the museum next door, Ronan Sinclair. There were a number of cardboard boxes by the door, and he was picking them up and taking them inside.

The man smiled. "I'm the curator here — well, curator, dogsbody, anything and everything that's required really."

He was a smartly dressed man, tall, with iron-grey hair. He was older than Calladine had imagined, his own age at least.

Ronan moved closer. "You don't look right. Want to come inside, get your breath back?"

Calladine did feel shaky, which wasn't like him at all. He nodded. He'd take a few minutes to recover and then get off home. "I've not been here in years," he said.

"We've moved on in recent times. We put on events and displays to attract the schools and bring in the locals. We're aiming to be the hub of the community. I think the museum is more popular now than it ever was."

"And you're getting the Hoard back, that'll cause some interest," Calladine said.

"It certainly will." He grinned. "Security will be a pain though. We had to spend money and go through hoops to satisfy the people in London before they'd let us have it."

"Worth it though. It'll bring in folk from all round Greater Manchester, not just locals."

Ronan Sinclair picked up one of the battered cardboard boxes left by the door and placed it on a table in the centre of the room. "The people around here bring us all sorts of things," he said. "They turn out their attics and drawers and imagine we'll be happy to find a home for all their old junk. I mean, what's this?"

Calladine looked at the object Sinclair held up and couldn't believe he'd asked the question. "You're joking, aren't you?"

Sinclair tossed it back in the box. "No, mate, I haven't a clue."

Calladine shoved his hands in his coat pockets, nodded a goodbye and left. The evening had been a disaster on the Kitty front and now he had something else to think about. Ronan Sinclair was a fraud.

CHAPTER 42

Day Six

"Question for you," he said to Ruth the following morning. "How come the curator of the local museum has no idea what a wooden pirn is?"

"A pirn?"

"You know, they used them in weaving. The bit you wind the woollen thread on to and stick into the shuttle. There's loads of them cluttering up the junk shops and car boots around here, along with other weaving paraphernalia."

"I know what they are," she said. "I'm trying to understand what you're getting at."

Without explaining, he turned to Alice. "Ronan Sinclair, the curator of Lowermill museum — find out how long he's been in post and where he came from."

"Is it important?" Ruth asked. "Only right now we've got the odd murder on our plates, among other puzzles."

"I think it's key, Ruth." Calladine disappeared into his office and shut the door behind him. An hour of quiet would do him good. They had the meeting with Julian later, and it was important he stay awake. When Julian was in full flow, he tended to drone. It could send anyone to sleep, tired or not.

Calladine had had a bad night going over the previous evening in his head. He should have tackled Kitty properly, asked her outright, but he'd wimped out. Understandable, he supposed. He liked her and didn't want to hurt her feelings. It was something he'd have to get over and quick, because if his theory was right, she was a killer. Then there was bumping into Sinclair and the conversation they had had. Then, sometime between three and four in the morning, he'd had a eureka moment.

Calladine believed he was right in his suspicion. This case wasn't about drugs at all. It might have been for Lazarov, but he was out of it now anyway. Calladine wanted more information to prove his theory before he discussed it with the team.

Alice knocked on the door and he beckoned her in. "I can't find a single trace of Karen Thornton, sir," she said.

"Forget her for the moment and concentrate on Sinclair. Oh, and do me a personal favour. Find out everything you can about Kitty Lake, the manager of the new restaurant in Lowermill, Mother's Kitchen, and keep it to yourself. Get anything, don't discuss it, come to me direct."

Alice nodded and left the room.

His mobile rang. It was Marilyn. "Sam has just growled at me again. Can you believe that? The way I used to spoil him, too. Ungrateful mutt."

"What d'you want, Marilyn?" he asked.

"You left this morning and never even said goodbye. I was hoping we could chat over breakfast and you might give me the grand tour, show me what's changed around here in my absence."

He didn't have time for this. Fine, she could stay, but no way was he entertaining or babysitting her. "Sorry, no time. Isn't there someone else you can bother?"

"Ray was right about you, you're rude and you've no time for anyone. Family has always come last where you're concerned. Are you aware that your attitude broke Freda's heart?"

"You know precious little about Freda and you're not family either," he snapped. "Neither was Ray, come to that."

"Rubbish. Freda raised the both of you. Now, where can I find Zoe? I'd like to have a look at that infant of hers."

"You're out of luck, they've gone away for a few days," he said.

"At this time of year and with a new babe? Won't be much of a break. Hard work if you ask me."

"Look, Marilyn, I've got to go, I've a mountain of stuff to get through. Catch you later."

Calladine finished the call and went to find Ruth.

"What's wrong with your face?" she asked.

"Marilyn's being a pain already," he said. "She thinks I've nowt better to do than run her around town."

"Fancy going down to the canteen for a coffee?" she asked. Not a bad idea, might help him stay awake.

"You look ropey again," she said on their way down.

"Lack of sleep and having Marilyn under my feet."

"Good night at Kitty's, was it?"

"No, I left early again."

"What is it with you and that woman? For reasons I can't fathom, she likes you, but the minute she tries to get close, you do one."

He ignored the comment. "D'you think you'd still recognize Millie Reed if you saw her today?"

She blinked. "I'm not with you."

"Suppose those aren't her bones. Suppose they belong to someone else. What if Millie came back to Leesworth for some reason? Would you know it was her?"

Ruth looked mystified. "I might, but I didn't know her that well in the first place and it's been a lot of years. Some folk don't change much, but others do." She gave him a funny look. "Why? What's going on?"

Calladine took a last swig of his coffee and helped himself to a biscuit. "You said Kitty deliberately ran into me that day on the Hobfield."

"She did. I saw it plain as day. It was no accident, Tom."

"She hasn't met you," he said thoughtfully. "Would you visit the restaurant this morning, Mother's Kitchen? Don't say

179

who you are, have a good look at Kitty, then come back here and tell me what you think."

Her eyes widened. Then she shook her head. "You're not serious. Surely you don't think Kitty Lake is Millie? When did you dream that one up?"

"I think it's a possibility and I want you to help me make up my mind. Not a word to the others, mind, or to Greco. For the time being, it's just between you and me."

CHAPTER 43

Ruth had just parked up in Lowermill and was crossing the road when she spotted Jake Ireson coming towards her. She and Jake had lived together as a couple and had a son, but were currently estranged. Several months ago, he'd had an affair with a colleague at the school where he taught and was now living with her. Initially, Ruth had been upset, then, realizing that they hadn't been getting on for a while, she resigned herself to the situation. But as the weeks passed, she began to think again. There was a time when she'd loved Jake, and if she was honest with herself, she'd like those times back.

"Ruth!" he called out. "I was going to ring you. Can we talk? Soon?"

She looked at him. He had that earnest look on his face, the one that smacked of him wanting something.

"Work, Jake. Remember that? Well, I'm up to my ears right now." She immediately regretted the put-off. Why, whenever she saw him face to face, did she always react this way? Orla Gray, that was why, and the fact that Jake had fallen so easily for her.

"Don't be so antagonistic towards me, Ruth. I only want a chat."

He had that little-boy-lost look, the one he did so well. Her resolve melted. She missed him and so did their son, Harry. She nodded at the Mother's Kitchen restaurant. "Okay. How about now? You can take me for a pot of tea in there."

"If that's what you want."

"I do and it's work, so no mention of me being a detective, got it?"

They found a table and sat down. "What's this about?" he whispered.

"I can't say, so don't ask. How's Orla?" A snide comment and another one she regretted. Oh well, she'd asked now. Ruth could see from his face that the question threw him. "I won't pretend she doesn't exist. After all, she's the reason you left us."

"Don't spare my feelings," he said. "Throw it all in my face why don't you."

"You didn't spare mine, Jake. You took off at a moment's notice, didn't give me or Harry a second thought as I recall."

"You're right, Ruth." He looked crestfallen. "I can't pretend Orla didn't happen. She came along when I was at a weak moment. I'm not making excuses, I was looking for something — change, anything, and there she was."

Ruth laughed. "Poor you, a weak moment. Couldn't help yourself I suppose. Not your fault at all, you just couldn't resist her."

"If you're going to be like this, I'm leaving you to it," he snapped.

"Like what?"

"Bitter, Ruth, and it doesn't suit you. We need to talk, properly, like adults. All this sniping will get us nowhere."

"Quiet, the waiter's here. Order the tea and let me look around."

Ruth saw a woman standing behind the reception counter who had to be Kitty. Ruth stood up, went over and asked for the ladies.

The woman was facing Ruth, so she had a good look at her. Beneath the dark hair, she saw high cheekbones and full lips. There was no mole now, but there was the faintest scar where it would have been.

"Well that sorts that," Ruth said. "Give me a moment and then we'll talk." Turning her back on Jake, Ruth took her mobile from her pocket and rang Calladine. "I can't be sure. There are similarities. Same height, and she does have a scar. The blonde hair's gone but that's easy enough to see to. Sorry, Tom, that's the best I can give you."

"Nothing certain, then?"

"I wish I could remember something definitive about her, apart from that mole, but I can't. For now, the jury is out." Ruth put her mobile back in her pocket and sat down opposite Jake. "Right then, how are we going to sort this?"

"I want you back," he said, surprising her. "You and Harry. I want us to be a family again."

"I'm not sure if I can trust you now, Jake," she said doubtfully. "You dumped us once, and for no other reason than a pretty face as far as I can see. You could do it again, and neither me nor Harry could take that. He's getting older. Soon he'll understand what's going on."

"This is no spur-of-the-moment thing, Ruth. I've lain awake nights thinking it over. I made a mistake. I was wrong and I deeply regret it. I want you back, simple as that."

His voice shook, he sounded emotional, which was unusual for him. She saw that he meant every word. This was decision time for Ruth. Part of her wanted to send him packing, pay him back for what he'd done to her, but what would that solve? She still loved him and so did Harry.

"Me and Harry need a commitment from you. So what do we get?"

"I won't do it again."

"Not good enough," she said. Ruth watched him. His hands were shaking so much he spilled sugar on the table. He was really nervous, obviously there was a lot riding on her response.

"Okay, I understand, and you're right," he said. "If we sort this, then we do it properly." He took her hand. "I mean, make it legal. Marry me, Ruth."

CHAPTER 44

Ruth was silent all the way to the Duggan. Calladine pulled into the car park and turned to her. "What's the matter? Is it the Kitty thing? You knew her once and I trust your judgement, which is why I asked."

"No, it's not that, though I do think your reasoning is a bit weird. Millie Reed is dead, Kitty has a scar on her face. You can't investigate every woman with a scar."

"Point taken, but I saw a photo in her flat of her as a young teenager. She looked very like the Reed girl, blonde hair and all."

"A lot of kids have blonde hair."

"Okay, we'll drop it for now. If not Kitty, what is it then? You're in a strange mood."

She was smiling. "I bumped into Jake. We went to the restaurant together, talked things through."

"About bloody time. Cleared the air between you I hope."

"Oh we did that all right. The short version is he's asked me to marry him."

Ruth got out of the car and crossed the tarmac ahead of him. Calladine was delighted. At last. Jake Ireson had taken long enough to get it together. He was glad he'd finally seen sense.

"Hold up," he called to her. "Before we go in, don't say a word to the others about the Kitty thing."

"Afraid you'll look foolish?" she said.

"No, well, perhaps. I'm still not sure."

"And you can keep my news just between us too. Deal?" Calladine nodded. "Once Julian has finished with us, you can tell me what's going on inside that head of yours and where these wild ideas about Kitty have come from."

"The photos started it," he admitted.

"They're old, Tom, taken at a distance and blurry. How can they tell you anything?"

"You think I'm mistaken?" he said.

"I do," she said, "and I hope that whatever mess you made of this fledgling relationship last night is repairable."

He shrugged. "We'll see."

"Marilyn behaving now?" she asked.

"I've no idea."

"Her turning up like this is very odd, don't you think? Where did she get the money for the appeal for starters?"

"I've no idea. Perhaps I should ask."

"Debra Weller is a partner in a firm of top-notch lawyers and doesn't come cheap, and then there's the barrister to pay for plus a load of other expenses. I thought Marilyn was broke. All Ray's money and goods were confiscated — proceeds of crime and all that."

Ruth was right. And Calladine hadn't even thought about it.

* * *

Calladine, Ruth, Rocco and Greco sat on one side of the table with Julian, Roxy and Natasha on the other. Julian handed each of them a document of several pages.

"I'll give you our findings in more detail, but I've summarized them for you while you're waiting for the official report," he said.

Roxy handed Calladine his mobile. "We have the number of the person who rang you — Lazarov you said. Needless to say, the phone was our old friend, a pay-as-you-go. I rang the number back yesterday and a man answered. He said only one word, 'yes'. I made up some tale about wanting to know train times. He cottoned on and finished the call pretty quick, but it was enough to ping the mast in Lowermill. I did try again but the number is no longer responding."

"Someone has Lazarov's phone and he's local," Calladine said.

"It would appear so," Roxy said.

"We've done a sweep of the workshop at Gorse House," Julian said. "We didn't find any prints on the freezer or the locks. I suspect they were wiped clean. There is evidence that someone has been camping out there. We found a sleeping bag and basic cooking equipment stashed under that bench. We also found a black bin bag full of rubbish — empty sandwich cartons, water bottles and beer cans. Initial DNA tests show that most of it was consumed by Lazarov. However, on one of the cans we found DNA that we have no match for."

That was something at least and might be the breakthrough they needed.

"Someone was up there with Lazarov," Julian said. "But I can't understand why he would choose that location as a hiding place. How would he know the place even existed?"

He was right. Calladine had also wondered what had prompted Lazarov to stay up there. Someone must have told him about the place, that was the only explanation.

"Remember, he was a wanted man," Ruth said. "He'd operated in this area before, so someone might have recognized him if he was seen around town."

"When you found him, Andrei Lazarov had been dead anywhere between thirty and forty hours," Natasha added.

"That makes it shortly after he rang me," Calladine said.

"He was shot," Natasha continued. "A single bullet between the eyes. We found it lodged in his skull."

"The bullet came from the same gun, a Glock, that killed the two young men," Roxy said. "So it could have been the same killer."

"Or Lazarov killed them and whoever shot him took his gun," Calladine said.

"Unfortunately, we found no prints at the flat where the lads were shot. We're still on the hunt for DNA that didn't belong to them, but the killer was careful. He left no hair, no blood, nothing," Natasha said.

"What about the workshop?" Calladine said.

"Same thing," Julian said. "The only prints and DNA belonged to Lazarov. The mud with the berry juice came from the land around Gorse House. There were patches on the workshop floor. I'm doing tests. If the composition proves to be the same as in the flat where the lads were shot, it suggests that whoever killed them had been in the vicinity of the house beforehand."

"I agree, Tom," Greco said. "It adds weight to the drugs war theory."

Only inasmuch as whoever killed Lazarov wasn't happy with what the Bulgarian had been up to. Perhaps he thought Lazarov's activities compromised his own. For now, Calladine didn't contradict him, he still needed proof of his alternative theory. Plus, it didn't solve the problem of how that same mud got into Becca O'Brien's flat.

"You're still searching?" he asked Julian.

"Yes, and the minute we get something, you will know."

That would do for now. Calladine got to his feet. "Thanks. That's all very useful." He rolled up Julian's report and stuffed it in his pocket. "I'll get back to the station, have a read through this."

CHAPTER 45

Calladine returned to his office and gave Julian's report a once-over. He was looking for evidence to prove Greco's theory wrong and that this case had nothing to do with drugs, but there was nothing of any help in the report.

His mobile rang and his heart sank when he saw Kitty's name on the screen. What could he say to her? He liked the woman, he wanted to make up and start again, but what if she was involved somehow? He couldn't shift the image of the girl in the school uniform.

He wimped out and didn't pick up the call. Within seconds he got a text: *I'm in the car park outside — join me or I'm coming in.*

His knees shaking, he peeped out of his office window. Her car was there below. This was stupid. He was a grown man for heaven's sake. He'd have to face her, tell her of his suspicions.

"I've got a visitor," he said to Ruth. "Kitty wants to see me. She's waiting in the car park."

"Need backup?" she teased.

Calladine said nothing. This was no joke. "What you said about Marilyn needing money to pay for her lawyers got me thinking. Would you check it out? I refused to listen to Debra Weller when she tried to explain why Marilyn had got parole, but she did say people had given evidence in court that they witnessed Ray's behaviour towards her. See if you can find out who they were."

Ruth shook her head. "It has no bearing on the current case. You sure we can spare the time and resources?"

"Do it for me, please," he asked. "If I can find a way of getting rid of that woman, I'll feel tons better. Now to face Kitty."

He walked across the tarmac and climbed into the car beside her. "Is this important?" he asked. "Only we've a lot on." He'd sounded short, almost angry, and he immediately wanted to apologize. Why could he never get it quite right with this woman?

"You've always a lot on, Tom, but yes, it is important. I think it's about time we introduced a little honesty into this relationship."

"Suits me."

"I've got a picnic in the boot," she said. "Well, a couple of sarnies and a flask of coffee. Where d'you suggest we go?"

"Gorse House," he said.

"You'll have to direct me, I've no idea where that is," she said.

"You sure? Because I think you might have lived there at one time."

Kitty turned and looked at him. "We'll go to the park. The sooner we sort this nonsense the better."

She drove the short distance to the park in silence. "Want to sit on a bench?"

"We'll stay in the car. I don't have long. Just say what's on your mind."

"I'll get the food out first."

Calladine couldn't eat anything, he felt sick with nerves. After last night, he was surprised that Kitty was even giving him the time of day. She went to the boot and came back with a pack of sandwiches and the coffee.

"I should have trusted you from the start. The way I've gone about things hasn't done me any favours. That bump I gave your car — it was deliberate."

He sipped at the coffee. "My colleague was watching, she said as much. Get to the point, Kitty."

"I did it for the best of reasons. You're a policeman and I thought I might need your help. It'd be easier if we already had a relationship, knew each other."

"You've been using me."

"As backup, if I had to, but that was at the beginning. Once I got to know you a bit better, I liked you for yourself. I thought we could have something. You did too, I could tell."

Calladine looked straight ahead. "I have to get back shortly, so get on with it."

"You're right, Tom, I am a fraud, I'm not who I say I am. The restaurant manager thing is a cover."

Here it was. "So who are you?"

"My name is Kitty Lake, or Katherine Lake in full. I know what you think, I've done my research. I can assure you that I am most definitely not the girl you think was murdered twenty-odd years ago come back to wreak some sort of revenge."

"You look like her and there's that scar on your face."

"Coincidence, nothing more. Do the checks, you'll see I'm telling the truth. Get your people to check out Katherine Lake, born in Cheadle, parents, Anne and Robert."

Calladine made a mental note to do exactly that once he got back. "Okay, if you're no restaurant manager, what are you?"

"A private investigator."

CHAPTER 46

Calladine wasn't sure what he'd been expecting, but it wasn't that. "I don't understand. Are you working on something now?"

"Yes. I'm investigating Ronan Sinclair," she said. "His wife hired the company I work for to find out if he's having an affair."

After meeting Sinclair last night, this made sense. He definitely wasn't who he said he was. "Who d'you work for?"

"Central Investigations in Manchester," she said. "I've been with them five years. "But it's a slog to be honest and I've fancied a change for ages. Since I've been in Leesdon, I've met a man called Sandy Cole. He's a PI with an office on the High Street."

"Yes, I know him."

"Sandy is retiring, and I've made him an offer for the business." She gave him a coy look. "That's partly why I made that clumsy move on the Hobfield. You're police and could be useful in the future. Sandy did mention your name."

Calladine shook his head. "You deliberately slammed into my car?"

"Well it wasn't really that bad, I only tapped it, you said as much yourself. I couldn't think of any other way to meet you."

"It would have been simpler to come to the nick and introduce yourself."

"True, but my way was a lot more fun." She grinned. "And I didn't want to blow my cover. For all I knew, you could have been best buddies with Ronan."

"Is Sinclair having an affair?"

"Yes. He's only been married a matter of months, too, but I've finally got the proof I need. I've been on his tail for a month now, but finally, this week she turned up. He's met up with her most days. I'm in the process of putting together my report for his wife. She asked him for a divorce but he refused point-blank. Told her she'd have to wait until the two years are up. She's not prepared to do that, wants rid of him so she can get on with her life. She'll be relieved, my report will give her the evidence she needs, but it's taken time and cost her a fortune."

She wasn't Millie Reed. At once, Calladine felt lighter. What a relief. Kitty's explanation made sense. "During the time you've been watching him, has anything struck you as odd?"

"He's no museum curator if that's what you mean," she said. "His wife said he worked in finance, at some bank in Manchester. I checked, but they've never heard of him. I suppose his wife will have to know that, too."

"Did you find anything to suggest that his name isn't Sinclair?" Calladine asked.

"No, he's who he says he is but he's faked his CV. He's spent most of his working life behind a bar in various pubs in Manchester, not what he told the interview panel for the museum job. He got that on false credentials, including a bogus degree from a university in London and fake references. I followed one of them up. It turned out to be a friend of his who was lying for him. When we met, he told me he left a museum job in Cheshire six months ago and got the job here in Leesworth shortly after that. Very different from what he told his wife, but it's all lies."

"No qualifications to do the job at all?" Calladine asked.

Kitty shook her head. "Just a very good con man. I reckon he's after the Hoard. If you think about it, it's the only explanation that makes sense. The pay he gets now is a pittance for the hours he works. He lives in Cheshire, so the job isn't even local. Plus, he talks of little else."

Calladine thought that idea a little far-fetched but said nothing. Instead, he leaned across and kissed her. "Thanks. You've made an old man very happy."

"In that case, do I get a reward? Supper later, perhaps?"

Calladine nodded. He'd like nothing better. "You do restaurant manager well," he said. "I'd never have guessed."

She winked. "I'm a PI, that's the whole idea."

* * *

Calladine returned to the station with a spring in his step, feeling better than he had in days. Sorting things out with Kitty had done him the world of good.

Alice followed him into his office. "Can I have a word? It's about that matter you asked me to follow up on."

"The Kitty thing?"

"She appears to be working undercover, sir. She's not a restaurant manager at all but a private investigator. I spoke to her employers earlier — Central Investigations in Manchester — and they confirmed her identity, sent me a photo and said she was here in Leesworth working on a case. She's the woman you were having dinner with the night you saw me and Rocco."

Calladine nodded. "Thanks, Alice. Kitty's just told me herself, but it's good to know it has been backed up so solidly. You can go back to looking at Ronan Sinclair now. That is probably not his real name though. He allegedly worked for a bank in Manchester prior to the museum."

Alice had no sooner disappeared than Ruth came in. "Get it sorted, then?"

"She's a private investigator on the trail of an adulterer, none other than Ronan Sinclair."

"I always thought he was shifty. I told Jake as much when he waxed lyrical about the bloke and his plans."

193

"I wouldn't mind knowing more about Sinclair's plans myself. D'you know what Kitty thinks?"

Ruth grinned. "Taking notice now, are we?"

"She thinks he's after the Hoard." He sat back and watched her consider this.

"It's possible. What d'you think?" she said at last.

"He knows little about local history, not interested I'd say, but he's in Leesdon for some reason and Kitty reckons the Hoard is the best bet."

Her eyes widened. "We have no proof of that, and anyway, it's a wild idea. What's your lady friend said? Does she have any evidence?"

"Kitty's after proof of adultery, that's all. His wife wants divorce without having to wait. Kitty is suspicious because she can't find any background beyond a few months ago."

"We should talk to the wife, make it official," Ruth said. "We can't allow all that Celtic gold to come here if there's the remotest chance of it being nicked."

CHAPTER 47

The lunchtime rush was over, but Mother's Kitchen was still busy. Kitty was back behind the counter serving food and drinks with a young man assisting.

"Have you got time for a word?" Calladine asked. He saw the look she gave Ruth.

"I remember you. You were in here, weren't you? You sat over there watching me. You had a damn good look and then reported back to this one, am I right?"

"His idea, Kitty, not mine," Ruth said with a grin. "Gets something stuck in his head and it takes some shifting."

"This is Ruth, she's my sergeant and friend," he said.

"Is he always like this?" Kitty asked.

"Fixated on mad ideas? Oh yes," Ruth said.

Kitty pointed a finger at Calladine. "I want you here at 8 p.m., no later. Bail and you won't enjoy the consequences. So, what d'you want now?"

"I wouldn't mind a look at the information you've gathered so far on Ronan Sinclair. If you're right about the Hoard, it gives us a problem. Knowing who he is involved with might help. And I think I should have a word with his wife. Can I have her address?"

"Give me a minute." Kitty disappeared upstairs and returned with a folder. "Everything I've got so far is in there, including his home address along with some recent photos of him with his woman." She gave him a warning look. "Don't lose anything. Copy what you need but I want them back this evening."

"Thanks, Kitty, we're very grateful." They went back to the car.

"She likes you," Ruth said. "You'll have to be careful, she's definitely another one who's fallen for the Calladine charm."

"Don't be stupid. I'm an old man. I'll be a phase. Young good-looking woman like her, it'll soon wear off."

He tossed Ruth the keys. "You drive. I'll have a look through Kitty's notes."

On the way back to the station, Calladine read through what Kitty had discovered about Sinclair. It made interesting reading, but what grabbed his attention the most were the photos.

Sinclair and a woman sitting together on a park bench. Both were smiling, and he had his arm around her. They looked easy in each other's company, like old friends or lovers. "Well, well. Sinclair's woman — guess who she is."

Ruth shrugged. "Wouldn't know where to start. I see him about, but other than that, I don't know the man."

"None other than Marilyn Fallon. That explains why she'd been so keen to stay with me."

"D'you think Sinclair and Marilyn are planning to steal the Hoard? Should we bring them in?" Ruth said.

"We don't know that's what he's here for yet. He might be an adulterer and ignorant of local history, but those aren't crimes."

"Marilyn was married to one of the most notorious villains going. She must have learned something. For all we know she could be the brains behind the whole thing," Ruth said.

"True, but we need evidence," Calladine said. "Anyway the Hoard isn't even here yet."

"It's arriving next week. The paper is full of it. There's to be a special viewing for local worthies and the press a week today," she said.

Calladine had returned to the notes. "Says here Sinclair visited Marilyn in prison a number of times. When we reach the station, find out how frequent those visits were and when they started. Kitty has only been keeping tabs on him for a month."

"Are you going to speak to Marilyn?" she asked.

"I'm not sure. I could do with more information first," he said. "We have to be certain we're right about the Hoard."

Ruth pulled into the station car park. "D'you intend to tell the others? Greco at least."

"No, I want to speak to Debra Weller first," he said. "For now this is between us."

"Okay, but it's no use telling folk after the Hoard has walked."

Ruth left him in his car, still looking at the photos, mostly taken in Leesdon park. He put the papers back in the folder. He wouldn't say anything to Marilyn for now. Better she was oblivious to the fact that Kitty was on Sinclair's tail and that he too was interested in him.

When Calladine went into the station, the duty sergeant told him there was a woman waiting to see him. "She's been here a while now — in there." He nodded to a side room.

"Does she have a name?" Calladine asked.

"Karen Thornton."

CHAPTER 48

"I believe you've been looking for me," Karen Thornton said.

"How did you know? Did someone tell you?" Calladine said.

"Sarah," she admitted. "I'm afraid she wasn't being honest when she told you we'd lost touch. Not her fault, I asked her to keep my whereabouts to herself. I left Leesdon years ago. My mother was thrown out of the flat we lived in, so that was that. She left owing some dangerous people, drug dealers mostly, a lot of money. I was afraid that if people discovered where I was, they'd come looking. I ended up working in a guest house in Whitby, got married and never had any reason to come back here. The only person I did keep in touch with was Sarah, and she told me what had happened."

"D'you have any ID to prove that?" he said. "I need to be sure that you really are Karen, and this isn't some ruse you or someone has concocted to confuse the case."

She rummaged in her bag and took out a passport. "That do you? It's still valid and has my photo on it."

Calladine took the document. It was in order. "Thanks for coming in. I wanted to speak to you about something that took place a long time ago up at Gorse House. Jade O'Brien was injured."

"Not just Jade." She grimaced. "I got a whack on the head too. That girl Millie was a nutjob, no other way of describing her. She had a vicious temper once she got going. There were three of us and we were hard cases ourselves, but we were no match for the bitch when she went mad with that hammer. She was like a rabid dog that day, chased us down the hill with that damn hammer in her hand. Jade was hurt bad, me not so much. I was lucky, I recovered. I thought no more about it until Sarah rang me."

"D'you know what happened to Millie Reed?" he asked.

"I know she ended up dead in a hole, but I've no idea how or why."

"Did any of you return later on, try to get even with the girl?" Calladine said.

"We were too scared, and Jade wasn't right. Besides, I had enough going on with our eviction. My mum needed me with her," Karen said.

It was a reasonable-enough account, similar to what others had told him. "Would you be willing to make a written statement of everything you've just told me?"

"Yes, of course. Anything to help."

Calladine went and got a uniformed PC to organize the statement. "Leave me a contact number and address before you go," he said. "There may be more questions."

* * *

Back in his office, Calladine rang Debra Weller. "Would it be possible to meet?"

"I'm not in Leesdon currently, I'm back in my office in Manchester. Is it important?" she said coldly.

"Yes, and it does concern Marilyn."

"I hope you're not planning a mudslinging fest, Mr Calladine. I heard from Marilyn only this morning, and she's doing fine."

"She is, I've no complaints on that score, but there is a rather delicate matter I'd like to discuss with you."

"I have an important case on my hands right now. When I've got a spare hour, I'll ring you but give me a day or so."

He'd have to be satisfied with that. Anyway, he needed time to gather as much evidence as he could get his hands on. Where the money came from to pay Marilyn's legal fee for starters, and the name of the person who'd backed her story about Ray's behaviour in court. He went out into the main office. Ruth wasn't there. Rocco and Alice were sitting together studying a screen of information. Rocco had his arm around her. They must have decided that now he knew, they didn't have to hide the relationship anymore.

Calladine cleared his throat. "Just as well I'm not Greco. Mind you, he can't talk. Alice, the parole hearing for Marilyn Fallon. Would you find me as much information as you can about the witnesses, names in particular? Also, fast-track all you can get on Ronan Sinclair. Find out about those visits to Marilyn in prison — how often, dates and so on." He handed her the name and address of Sinclair's wife. "Ring this woman, too, find out when she met Sinclair and how much she knows about his history."

"Isn't Marilyn Fallon the woman staying with you, your cousin's wife?" Rocco asked.

"Yes, she is, and I'm beginning to smell a rat." He checked his phone — late afternoon already. "I'm getting off. Alice, find anything, give me a ring."

An early finish would do no harm. He'd go home and get ready for tonight and his date with Kitty. He was glad he'd been wrong about her. Now he'd be free to see a lot more of her if she intended to stay on in Leesdon. For the first time in a while, life felt good.

Out in the fresh air he inhaled deeply, and then rubbed his chest. He'd had a niggling pain for days, made worse when he got out of breath or stressed. He really should get it seen to. Ruth had noticed. Perhaps, when the case was finally sorted, a word with Doc Hoyle would do no harm.

CHAPTER 49

"I'll be submitting my report to Sinclair's wife within the next couple of days," Kitty said. "I've got all the evidence she's asked for. Once that happens, I leave Mother's Kitchen, too, and will have to find somewhere else to live."

"Sandy Cole has his offices on the ground floor but there's a flat upstairs. What about that?" Calladine said.

"It's got a sitting tenant," she said. "I got a good deal on the property because of it. I spent most of my spare cash buying Sandy out, so I hope the bank will be generous. I have an appointment in the morning to chat about how much of a mortgage I can get. I'm just hoping it's enough to buy one of those houses by the canal."

"If all else fails, you can have my spare room." Calladine smiled.

"You've got Sinclair's other woman in it," she said.

"Not for much longer if things go according to plan," he said.

They were sitting together on the sofa. Kitty took his hand. "I'd like nothing better, but wouldn't it be rushing things a bit? Up until yesterday, you thought I might be a murderer, now you're offering me a room in your home."

"I'm really sorry for my suspicions. Can we drop it now, please? The whole Millie Reed thing gives me the shivers," he said.

"She has increased your workload," Kitty said. "As well as everything else, you're having to find out who killed her."

Calladine hadn't really thought about it but she was right, and particularly if those bones Julian was testing confirmed it was Millie. He couldn't see who else they'd belong to. Jade, Karen and Sarah were all accounted for.

Kitty smiled at him. "This is something of an event. We've actually managed an entire meal without you dashing off."

He moved closer. "Let's hope there'll be many more."

"What're you doing about the Hoard? Are you letting it come here or what?" she asked.

Calladine spread his hands out. "I need concrete evidence that it's in danger of being stolen before I can stop it. Tomorrow, with luck, I'll have enough to speak to my DCI, get him onside and go from there."

"Sinclair is a fraud, you said so yourself, and the woman he's taken up with has just come out of prison for killing her husband. They have to be planning something, they've got the right background."

"I didn't like Ray much, but it was heartless of her to kill him like that, in cold blood. I reckon Marilyn is capable of anything. It wouldn't surprise me if she was the brains behind the plans to steal the Hoard." But where did Lazarov fit into all this? Sinclair and Marilyn were one thing, but the Bulgarian was a drugs man.

"I doubt Ronan could plan anything," Kitty said. "The man's an idiot. He behaves like a lapdog around that woman. She's been with him most days and has stayed over several times. The other night they had a late one, a couple of his friends came round, and they were laughing and chatting until the small hours. The following morning he knocked on my door asking for coffee. I took some round and found your Marilyn and some stray bloke comatose on the sofa."

How had Marilyn organized a big operation like this? And how had she met Sinclair in the first place? As far as Calladine knew, he'd had nothing to do with Leesworth or the museum until a few months ago. Someone must have approached him — and it couldn't have been Marilyn, she was in prison — knowing he'd be up for whatever Marilyn had in mind. Was that Lazarov's doing?

Calladine hoped that Alice's research and whatever he learned from Debra Weller when she finally agreed to meet him, would give him some answers. The Leesworth Hoard and what might happen to it was one thing, but he had four murders on his plate and sorting them had to come first. The shootings of Lazarov and the two lads — was that down to another dealer? But who? No one Calladine had in his sights fitted the bill. And then there was the puzzle of Becca O'Brien's murder. That one was personal, all his instincts told him so, but again they had no evidence. Nothing but suspicions.

CHAPTER 50

Day Seven

The evening with Kitty did Calladine the world of good. He got home late and had a good night's sleep. He didn't hear Marilyn come in. It wasn't until the following morning that he realized she wasn't around. Marilyn had stayed out all night.

He'd mention it to Debra Weller the next time they met. He wasn't sure what the terms of her parole were, but it wouldn't do any harm to ask. A quick walk with Sam, a light breakfast and then he made for the station.

Alice greeted him with a smile. "Some of the info you wanted is on your desk, sir. I had to dig deep to find it but Sinclair's real name is Ronan Leyland, and he has a record for petty theft. He did a stint inside, too. As for the legal fees Mrs Fallon paid, we need a warrant to get access to her bank account. But my research did throw up something interesting."

Fair enough, he'd expected as much.

"The main witness, a woman purporting to have been close to Mrs Fallon, told the court how badly Ray treated her. She quoted dates and had photos of bruises he inflicted. She said she befriended Mrs Fallon and encouraged her to open up about it. According to her, she had witnessed Mr Fallon's cruelty towards his wife on a number of occasions. The witness said that several times she was concerned for her own safety, and eventually persuaded Mrs Fallon to ask for help."

"Is there any evidence that Marilyn did that?"

"No. Her husband was arrested and that was that."

"Who was this witness who perjured herself so expertly for Marilyn?" he asked.

"This is the interesting bit, sir. Her name is Maggie Cox, she's a physio at the hospital in Manchester. She's also—"

"I know who she is." Calladine smiled. "You've done well, Alice. Thanks."

Now he knew who the third man was — Lazarov, had to be. He had been living with Maggie Cox prior to his disappearance. Calladine wrote the name "Maggie Cox" on his notepad. He grabbed his coat and went into the main office. "Is Ruth about? I want the address for Maggie Cox."

With a smile, Rocco handed him a slip of paper. "Want me to come with you?"

As he spoke, Ruth entered the office with two cups of coffee. "One of these is for you."

"You stay here," he said to Rocco, "and bring Greco up to date. Ruth's already met the woman and knows the way there. While you're talking to Greco, get him to authorize a warrant to go through all the bank accounts held by Maggie Cox and Marilyn Fallon. Give him the gist and say to make it urgent. I want to know how much money they've both got stashed away and their spending pattern over these last few months." He nodded at the coffees Ruth was holding. "Fetch them with you, we're going for a ride into town."

* * *

Ruth had been to Maggie Cox's home before and knew where to park the car, so she drove.

"What's she like?" Calladine asked.

"Seemed okay to me," she said, "helpful enough. She told us Lazarov had left a month before and hadn't come back."

"Did she seem bothered about it?"

"Actually no, now that you ask," Ruth said.

Maggie answered the door and eyed Ruth warily. "I told you all I know the other day."

"Not quite, Ms Cox," Calladine said. "You didn't say anything about Marilyn Fallon and her connection to Lazarov."

As soon as he mentioned Marilyn, she stepped back as if about to shut the door in their faces. "I don't know anyone with that name."

"Odd that, because you were the main witness at her appeal. You stood up in court and told everyone how she was mistreated by her husband, Ray. You made a good job of it, too. Marilyn was released."

"What of it?" she shrugged, "Giving evidence isn't a crime."

"It is if it's false." Calladine smiled. "And it's not true, is it, Ms Cox? You lied in court and I believe you were paid a large sum of money to do so."

"Prove it!" she spat. "Now leave me alone. I don't want you coming to my house again."

"It doesn't work like that," Calladine said. "You're coming to Leesdon Police Station with us. You will be cautioned and then you will tell us exactly how you became involved with Lazarov and Marilyn Fallon."

"I want a solicitor."

"You can have one. Any preference?" he said.

"Debra Weller."

Calladine ushered Maggie Cox to the car. She sat in the back seat with Ruth while he drove. She'd asked for Debra Weller — why? Was she part of it? Had she been paid off too? He hoped not, because that would give them a problem. What he needed now more than anything was someone to tell the truth.

CHAPTER 51

Maggie Cox was put in an interview room with a uniformed officer to watch her. "Debra Weller, the woman she's asked for, is Marilyn's solicitor," Calladine told Ruth. "We'll delay, tell her Debra can't be reached."

"Julian's been on," Rocco told them. "He reckons he's got something for you."

Calladine rang him.

"D'you recall the empty drink cans we found in the workshop at Gorse House?" Julian said. "We've been through the lot, which was no mean task I can tell you. Most had evidence of Lazarov's DNA as you would expect, but one didn't. An empty lager can, two lots of different DNA and a trace of lipstick."

"What does that mean?"

"That the drink was shared by a man and woman, and recently, too — the saliva was relatively fresh."

Perhaps whoever killed Lazarov was having a small celebration. "Have you analysed it?" Calladine said.

"Of course. One set belongs to a Ronan Leyland and the other to Marilyn Fallon. A simple job — their DNA is on record."

Calladine couldn't stop beaming. "Julian, you're a wonder."

The scientist cleared his throat modestly. "Simply doing my job, Tom."

This was the breakthrough Calladine had prayed for. Marilyn and Sinclair — or Leyland to give him his real name — must have killed Lazarov and stuffed him in that freezer.

He needed those warrants for the bank accounts urgently. With the evidence he had, plus any suspect money transfers, Marilyn would be back inside by nightfall. He went for a word with Greco, to bring him up to date and get him to ring the magistrate. The DCI had more clout than him.

Greco onside, he returned to the main office to tell the others.

"The minute you hear that the magistrate has issued the warrants, check Cox's and Marilyn's accounts and text me the details," he told Ruth.

"Where are you going?" she asked.

"I'm going to arrest Marilyn. I want to know what she was doing up at Gorse House." He looked at Rocco. "You go and fetch Sinclair."

Outside the station, Calladine turned up his coat collar. It was raining and cold. Winter was starting. If it followed the usual pattern for these parts, it would be long and hard. He shivered, climbed into his car and turned the heater on full blast. He rang his home number and Marilyn answered. Good, no need to search around Leesworth for her.

"Stick the kettle on, I'll be back for a bite shortly." Better keep it friendly. He didn't want her doing a runner.

* * *

It took only minutes to reach his home. He checked his mobile — nothing. He hoped those bank details wouldn't take long. Proof of financial transactions between her and Cox, or her and Lazarov for that matter, would be the icing on the cake.

"Not like you to take time out," she said. "I've made a pot of tea. Had something to eat? I can get you a sandwich."

"Sorry, Marilyn, this isn't a social visit. I'm here to take you down to the station."

She looked confused. "Why? What on earth d'you think I've done?"

"How long have you known Ronan Sinclair — or Leyland to give him his proper name?"

"Long enough. This isn't about him, is it?"

Hearing the doorbell ring, Calladine looked out of the front window and saw Stephen Greco. What did he want?

"I've looked at the bank account, Tom. You were right to be suspicious," Greco said. Then, more quietly, "I'm arresting Marilyn Fallon. You are a relative, so you'll have to back off."

Calladine wanted to explain that she was no kin of his, Ray neither, but Greco was right, she was living under his roof. "I was just about to bring her in."

"Leave her to me. I've got a car and two uniformed officers to escort her."

"Sorry, Marilyn," Calladine said. "Get your coat. My colleague is here to arrest you."

CHAPTER 52

Marilyn Fallon was in an interview room with a uniformed officer, waiting for her solicitor to arrive. "She's asked for Debra Weller," Greco told Calladine.

"She's good," Calladine said. "She knows Marilyn and will have all the right bricks in place in no time. That woman got Marilyn off a murder charge on appeal, but what she doesn't realize is that she was conned. Once she knows the truth, we can only hope that Ms Weller isn't so keen."

Greco handed Calladine some paperwork. "The bank statements are all in there, plus other details of the accounts that you should be aware of. I'll deal with Fallon with Ruth, you and Rocco interview Maggie Cox."

Ruth came along the corridor to join them. "Debra Weller's arrived and she's not happy. She's in with Marilyn now, going over stuff."

Greco nodded. "It'll be you and me with Fallon."

"And you?" Ruth asked Calladine.

"I'll take Maggie Cox."

Greco led the way to the interview room. Marilyn and Debra Weller were deep in conference.

"This is one huge mistake," the solicitor said at once. "She had no idea what Ronan Sinclair was up to."

"I think Mrs Fallon knew very well what was going on," Greco said. He turned to Marilyn. "We have evidence that puts you and Sinclair at the scene of a murder. So why not save us all a lot of time and say what it was you and Sinclair were up to."

"Not me — Ronan," she said. "He planned to steal the Leesworth Hoard. That's why he got the job at the museum."

Greco nodded. "That much seems straightforward. But why start a relationship with you? What did he need you for? With his job, he was already well placed to do it on his own."

Marilyn said nothing to this. Greco checked his notes. "He even visited you in prison. Did you know the man prior to being convicted of your husband's murder?"

"No," she snapped. "Ronan came to see me out of the blue."

"I don't believe you. I think he knew you because he used to work for your husband, Ray. Ronan Leyland wasn't your only visitor either."

"True, a few people came to see me — Tom, for one. He asked me about people Ray had worked with too."

"I'm not talking about Tom Calladine," Greco said. "We've done our research, looked at the visitors' log and the CCTV footage." Marilyn's face fell. "Maggie Cox visited you too, more than once. We believe she was working for Lazarov, and that she was relaying messages between the pair of you. He couldn't visit himself because he was a wanted man, West Yorkshire's most prolific drug dealer. So he sent the woman he was living with to see you instead. What did he want, Mrs Fallon?" Debra Weller looked genuinely confused — she obviously had no knowledge of any of this.

"It was all his idea, Lazarov's," Marilyn said. "He planned to steal the Hoard and he hired me and Ronan to help him."

Greco dismissed that straight away. "That's a lie. Lazarov was a drug dealer. He had no interest in the Hoard, I doubt he even knew of its existence. You were the one who instigated the visit. You sent his girlfriend a visiting order. Why?"

"Ronan told me to."

Greco ignored her comment. "This is what I think happened. Lazarov had no interest in the Hoard, but he was interested in you, Mrs Fallon. You asked for the visit and dangled the prospect of getting even with Tom Calladine in front of him as a way to get him onside."

"Another of Ronan's ideas. He knew Lazarov had the money and the contacts to get me out. This entire thing is down to Ronan, surely you see that. He's the one who runs the museum where the Hoard will be kept. He's been planning this for months."

"If stealing the Hoard was Sinclair's idea, that still doesn't explain where you come in," Greco said.

She said nothing.

"I think the theft was your idea, Mrs Fallon. You used Tom Calladine as bait to lure Lazarov back to the area. You know a lot about him, including where he and his family live. What was the plan? Get Lazarov into Calladine's house late one night and stand by while he killed the man? You used Tom as bait and you're using Sinclair to get access to the Hoard."

Marilyn glared at him, tight-lipped.

"Why did you kill Lazarov? Outlive his usefulness, did he?"

"I didn't kill him," Marilyn protested. "We found him like that. When we'd left him the day before, he was fine. He must have upset someone, but it wasn't us. All he had to do was stay put, but he couldn't, could he? He wanted his business back, to be the top dog again."

"So, if that was the case, where did he go?" Greco asked.

"I'm not sure, we didn't follow him around. But I suspect he went into Leesdon at night, to the Hobfield. He upset someone, it's as simple as that."

Greco said nothing. He could see that Debra Weller was becoming more confused as the interview proceeded. He placed a sheet of paper in front of them both. "This shows a number of bank transfers. They're from an account owned by 'Andrei Holdings' to your account, Mrs Fallon. The amount is exactly what you needed to cover the legal fees for your appeal, isn't that so?"

Marilyn nodded.

"This transfer here is from 'Andrei Holdings' to an account belonging to Maggie Cox. She was the main witness at your appeal and the go-between for you and Lazarov. Am I right?" She nodded again. "'Andrei Holdings' is Andrei Lazarov, Mrs Fallon. He parted with a lot of money. He had to have had a good reason for doing that." He waited, but she remained silent. "Lazarov needed help to return to Leesworth, he was a wanted man. Walk the streets and he'd be inside within the hour. What he needed was a place to stay hidden and people to help him re-establish his business this side of the Pennines, make him untouchable once again. That was the deal, wasn't it? You gave him Tom Calladine and a secret hideaway, and he gave you money to fight your appeal."

Greco glanced at Debra Weller. She had a face like thunder. From her expression, the extent to which she'd been duped had just dawned on her, and she was furious.

Abruptly, she stood up. "Sorry, I can't do this." She turned to Marilyn. "You used me, all through the appeal and beyond. Even now you're still treating me like a fool. I believed you, I really thought you were a broken woman." She took hold of her things and made for the door. "Get someone else, Marilyn. I'm done with you."

Greco raised his eyebrows. "We'll leave this for now. We'll arrange another solicitor and resume later."

"You're making a huge mistake," Marilyn said. "You should go after the real villains, find out who really killed Lazarov because it wasn't me or Ronan."

Greco didn't reply. He and Ruth left the room. "Do we believe her, sir?" Ruth said. "We didn't ask her about the freezer or what happened to the gun."

"All in good time, Ruth. The woman needs time to consider her position. She's playing us. She's good, too, I'll give her that, but she's guilty all right. What we have to do is find out which one is the brains behind the plan to steal the Hoard, Marilyn or Ronan Sinclair, and who pulled the trigger."

"Lazarov not behind the plan, then?" she asked.

"No, Ruth. I think he helped obtain Marilyn's release in order to get at Tom. All he wanted was his drug business back, to see it up and running again. He planned to blackmail Tom into helping him by threatening his family."

"Why kill Lazarov?" she asked.

"Who knows, but don't worry, we'll find out."

CHAPTER 53

Calladine and Rocco sat down opposite Maggie Cox and her solicitor. "First, I want to discuss your relationship with Marilyn Fallon," Calladine began.

"She was my friend," Cox said.

"How did you become friends? You didn't live near her and Ray."

She shrugged. "I can't recall how, we just did."

"Fortunately, I know exactly how the pair of you met up," Calladine said. "She sent you a visiting order when she was in prison. Up until then, the two of you had been complete strangers."

"That's a lie, I did know her," Cox said.

"Marilyn wanted to contact Andrei Lazarov. Being a wanted man, he couldn't visit, so you went instead. What did you discuss?"

Maggie Cox looked him in the eye. "You!" she hissed. "Lazarov was obsessed with you. He wanted to get even, make you suffer for getting in his way."

"And there was me the hot topic in prison circles and I never knew." Calladine chuckled.

"It's no joke, Inspector. Lazarov wanted you dead. You ruined the Manchester side of his business. It was doing nicely until you interfered. He was making a fortune, which he lost thanks to you, and he wanted to get even."

"He was running a county lines operation and encroaching on my patch. What did he expect me to do? How did Marilyn know to send you the visiting order?"

"Someone Lazarov knows got a message to her," Cox said.

"You visited, and Marilyn was only too happy to offer me up in exchange for her freedom. Nice, and there's me giving the woman a roof over her head."

"She uses everyone, you should know that by now," she said.

"She wanted out and Lazarov wanted me, so where does Ronan Sinclair and the Leesworth Hoard feature in all this?"

Maggie Cox shrugged. "I've no idea. All Lazarov wanted was his business back. He tried, too. He was well on the way to making his presence felt on that bloody estate when he disappeared."

"Why the Hobfield in particular?" Rocco asked.

Cox nodded toward Calladine. "Because it would piss him off. He threatened you, didn't he?" she said to Calladine. "Got to you through your daughter and her kid. He was planning to kill them, too. He reckoned that would finish you for good."

Calladine shuddered. She was right, it would have. "You hid Lazarov," he said, "kept him safe from the police while he organized his new life. The man you were living with, Ms Cox, was a murdering drug dealer who you knew was a palpable threat to me and my family."

"I daren't say anything," she said. "He'd have killed me."

"He paid you a lot of money to lie for Marilyn. You were the main witness at her appeal. It was a good act you put on. Debra Weller was royally taken in."

"I'd no idea what was going on," Cox said. "What was I supposed to do? As I said, Lazarov would have killed me if I'd refused to do what he wanted."

"We'll leave it for now," Calladine said.

"Can I go?" Cox asked.

"No, you'll be staying with us."

* * *

Back in the main office, Calladine and Ruth discussed their respective interviews. "Maggie Cox is a right piece of work," Calladine said. "She knew Lazarov wanted to kill Zoe and the infant and did nothing about it."

Ruth handed him a mug of coffee. "It didn't work though, did it? You got them safely out of the way. Marilyn's having a meltdown. Now that Debra Weller knows the truth, she's done one, so it's the duty solicitor for Marilyn."

"Marilyn and Cox are one thing, but we mustn't forget Sinclair's part in all this," he said.

"He's been brought in too," Ruth said. "He's in interview room three."

"Good. I need to decide who really is the brains behind all this. Not Lazarov, for a start. It seems all he was interested in was restoring his drug-dealing business and getting back at me."

"Greco and I are having another go at Marilyn shortly."

"Okay, I'll take Sinclair. When you speak to Marilyn, find out where she and Sinclair met. I think it's important."

"I had a word with his wife, sir," Alice said. "She actually doesn't know much about him. Whirlwind romance, she said. Got married within three months of meeting. She said things started to go downhill shortly after the wedding. She knew marrying him was a mistake and wanted out. When he got the museum job and stopped going home it was a relief. By that time she was already suspicious that he'd been lying to her about any number of things. That's when she hired Ms Lake."

"Thanks, Alice." Calladine went into his office and closed the door behind him. He needed to speak to Zoe, make sure everything was okay.

She answered almost straight away. "Dad. You all right?"

"Yes, love. I was calling to find out about you. It'll all be over soon, and then you can come home. How's Maisie doing?"

"She's fine, enjoying being fussed over by the lot of us. She seems to have taken to Amanda — she's got a knack with babies."

"There's been no problems? Odd visits? Phone calls?"

"Nothing at all. This call from you is the only one we've had. You need to chill, Dad. This place is so out of the way, it's perfectly safe."

"I'll come and get you at the first opportunity," he said. "See you soon."

He missed them. The thought of what might have happened if Lazarov's plans had worked out terrified him. The teddy bear, the liquid thrown into the pram, they were leading up to something too dreadful to contemplate. He went back to join the others.

"Right, let's get this wrapped up. I want an end to it, and I want the ringleader," he said with a nod at Ruth.

"Before you disappear, Julian's been on," Ruth said. "He'd like a word."

Calladine disappeared back into his office and rang him. He hoped this wasn't about Zoe. He could only hold off telling him the truth for so long.

"The mud on the floor in Becca O'Brien's flat," Julian began.

Wrong case, but Julian sounded keen. "What about it?"

"We've been over that floor thoroughly. There was the bloody print near the wall, which you know about, but the only other one of any use was a muddy print by the door. It was big, made by someone wearing heavy shoes with distinctive soles."

"Does it match up with anything you got from Higgs?"

"No, bigger feet, so not Higgs. The print matches up with the shoes Lazarov was wearing when you found him."

"You sure?"

"Yes, Tom. That print was made by Lazarov. He was in that flat the night O'Brien was killed."

CHAPTER 54

Greco and Ruth resumed their interview with Marilyn, while Calladine and Rocco went to question Sinclair. The news about Lazarov had Calladine thinking. Why visit Becca? Neither Jade nor Johnno had seen any mud on the floor, or left any behind, so Becca must have already been dead when Lazarov went in. He pushed it to the back of his mind for the time being. Sorting this little lot came first. He'd deal with Becca's murder once that was done.

"How did you meet Marilyn Fallon?" Calladine asked Sinclair.

"I knew her from before," he said.

"Before what? Before she was locked up for killing her husband?" Calladine said.

"That's a bit harsh considering the result of the appeal."

"It is true, though, regardless of how you wrap it up," Calladine said. "Marilyn did kill Ray, and in cold blood, too. So, come on, when did you meet?"

"I can't remember, it was a while ago."

"Okay. When did you change your name from Leyland?" Calladine said.

He looked surprised. Surely, he must have realized they'd find out.

Calladine consulted the notes Greco had given him. "You have a record — petty theft mostly, but you did do a stint in prison."

"So, I was a naughty boy. I've grown up since then and I've changed."

"You were in prison with Ray, Marilyn's husband," Calladine said. "It's written here in my notes, so I'm thinking that's when you first met her, on one of her visits."

"Could have been. Can't remember," Sinclair said.

"Marilyn got Lazarov to fund her appeal, and in return the pair of you found him a place to hide in Leesdon — near me. But things didn't work out, did they? The villain got ambitious, started going out nights."

"He wanted his business back," Sinclair admitted. "Marilyn didn't want that, not yet anyway."

"Who killed those lads on the Hobfield?" Calladine said.

Sinclair shrunk back in the chair. "What lads? It wasn't me. I can assure you. I've never killed anyone, murder's not my style." His hands were shaking.

"Okay, if not you, then who? They were executed, Ronan, strapped to chairs and shot between the eyes."

Sinclair winced. "It was Lazarov. A warning to any others who felt like grabbing a share of the turf. He wanted rid of the competition. Those lads took no notice, so they became a lesson for anyone else who had the same idea."

Those lads had had a loose association with Johnno Higgs. He'd been damn lucky to survive. Odd that, he was well known. "How did Marilyn react to the shootings?"

"She went berserk. Said he had to go."

"Did she kill him?"

"I don't know," Sinclair replied, lowering his gaze. "All Marilyn really wanted was the Hoard, just enough of it to ensure she'd never want for anything again. She had a buyer, too — some bloke in the Far East. She'd done all the ground-work. It could have succeeded, if it hadn't been for Lazarov. Right from the start, Marilyn said he was a liability and a threat to our plans."

"Once he was out of the way, Marilyn had everything in place, didn't she?" Calladine said. "The curator of the local museum eating out of her hand, no more Lazarov, and me running round in circles chasing my tail. I'd say Marilyn makes a damn good villain. Mind you, she had a good teacher."

"As I said, I don't know if she did kill him," Sinclair said. "And if she did, I can't think when. We've been together most of the time since she got out."

"I know. Were you aware that your new wife is having you watched? She wants a divorce. How would Marilyn react to being named on the petition? I reckon it's you she'll be gunning for next."

"We found him dead on the floor of that workshop up at the house," Sinclair said.

"When?"

"Remember when I spoke to you on the street after you left Kitty's? I was taking those boxes into the museum. It was earlier that day. We went up that morning to check on him and found him lying on the floor. At first, Marilyn thought he was sleeping but he was dead all right, shot in the head."

Something occurred to Calladine, but he needed a quick word with Natasha before he acted on it. She'd given him an estimate for the time of Lazarov's death, but he wondered if she could narrow it down. He left the interview room and went to ring her.

He was in luck. Natasha had done more tests. "There's still a margin of error, Tom," she said. "You found him on the Friday morning at about eleven. I'd say he was shot on the Wednesday night."

Yes, Calladine realized, the timeline checked out. Certainly, there was no possibility of an earlier time of death because he'd spoken to Lazarov that Wednesday — on his way back from dropping Zoe at the safe house.

"Thanks, Natasha, that helps."

That was the night the lads had been shot, Calladine realized. Had Lazarov shot them and Marilyn lost it? Was that it? Something Kitty had said struck him. He took his mobile and rang her. "You told me that there was a night Marilyn stayed over with Sinclair," he began.

"She stayed over a few times before she moved in with you," she said.

Calladine wondered why that hadn't been picked up — the woman was on parole. "The night they made a noise, had people over and you found them the next morning. When was that?"

"It was a Wednesday night. They made such a din that I went round on Thursday morning to make sure they were okay. I ended up feeding them coffee. Mind you, they recovered pretty fast. I went round about seven thirty with the coffee, and an hour later I saw them go off together in his car."

"Thanks, Kitty, well remembered. On the one hand what you've just told me was helpful, but on the other, you've just given me a huge problem."

CHAPTER 55

Calladine asked the team, including Greco, to meet him in the main office. There, he said, "I've just confirmed with the Duggan that Lazarov was shot on the Wednesday night. Sinclair denies that they killed him and reckons they have alibis." He waited for their reactions.

Greco looked puzzled. "Marilyn denied the murder too," he said.

"They were partying with a couple of friends in the flat above the museum. I'll get their names and they can be interviewed. If everything checks out, that means we still don't have Lazarov's killer."

"I was so sure it was her," Greco said. "She's a strong woman, and in my opinion, quite capable of killing."

"She is. Marilyn did for Ray," Calladine said. "I'll speak to Sinclair some more and get the names of the people who were there that night. If the pair didn't kill Lazarov or the lads and haven't actually stolen the Hoard yet, you'll have to have a think about what charges we might level against them."

"Marilyn Fallon won her appeal on the basis of perjury. That'll do to start with," Greco said. "Maggie Cox was an accomplice."

223

"And Sinclair?"

Calladine saw the look on Greco's face. "Fraud. He faked qualifications and got the job at the museum on false pretences."

* * *

"Ronan, I'm inclined to believe you about not killing Lazarov." Calladine passed him a pen and paper. "Write down the names of all the people who were in your flat that Wednesday night."

"Will you speak to them?" Sinclair asked.

"Oh yes. We want chapter and verse. Your freedom depends on it."

Sinclair returned the paper with the names on it, and Calladine handed it to a uniformed officer. "Give that to DC Rockliffe straight away."

He turned back to Sinclair. "You said you found Lazarov dead, shot in the head. Tell me more about that."

"We turned up early that morning, we were taking him some supplies. We went into the workshop and there he was, dead on the floor. Marilyn reckoned he'd been there all night."

"What did you do?" Calladine asked.

Sinclair looked sheepish. "We hid him," he mumbled. "We bundled him into an old freezer and covered it with a tarpaulin. Marilyn said it could be years before anyone found him."

"What about the gun?" Calladine asked.

"No idea. We didn't find it."

"You're sure, Ronan? Marilyn didn't take it?"

Sinclair shook his head emphatically. "Not her style."

"Why Gorse House?" Calladine said.

"That outbuilding, the old workshop. It's abandoned but still in good nick. No one ever goes up there, the locals think it's haunted. More important, there's only one road up, and that only goes to the workshop, so no one uses it, no point."

"Whose idea was it to go there?"

"Mine. We needed somewhere for Lazarov to lie low. He was to help us get the Hoard and then leave the country — well, that was the plan anyway."

"Didn't work out that way though, did it? Lazarov has always been a dealer and the Leesworth area was going begging, just waiting for someone like him to move in. He couldn't help himself."

"Marilyn was always telling him to rein it in, but he sneaked off at night, stalked that bloody estate under cover of darkness. He set up a small network, forced people to work for him. Marilyn was scared that if he was caught, he'd talk, tell you lot what we were planning. When he shot those kids, it was the final straw. I know Marilyn had had enough, but it really wasn't us who killed him."

"Do you know if he was ever followed back to the workshop after these excursions?"

"I think he was, but I only know about the one instance," Sinclair said. "I didn't dare say anything to Marilyn, she'd have hit the roof."

"D'you know who it was?"

"No, just that he was young. I'd gone up there at the crack of dawn to take Lazarov some supplies. I caught a glimpse of him, hiding among the trees."

"Thanks, Ronan, you'll be staying with us for now. We'll talk again later."

CHAPTER 56

When Calladine returned to the main office, Rocco was waiting for him.

"Sinclair's alibis check out, sir," he said. "Apparently, they were playing poker until the small hours and crashed there because they'd drunk too much. One of the blokes who stayed over was the local mayor. I'd say that was pretty cast-iron."

"Well, if neither Sinclair nor Marilyn left his flat the night Lazarov was killed, it can't have been them. Frankly, I'm all out of ideas," Calladine admitted. "This case is doing my head in. I was so sure we had them. What about Julian? Have we heard anything from him?"

Rocco shook his head. "Who else could have done it? There's no one on the radar."

"Sinclair told me he saw someone hanging around in the woods," Calladine said. "He reckons that whoever it was followed Lazarov up from town. The villain had taken to hanging out on the Hobfield after dark."

"That's not what Johnno Higgs said," Rocco reminded him. "You too, remember? All was quiet, you said, no sign of any dealing."

Calladine sat down. "First there was dealing activity and then there wasn't. I decided it was a sham, someone out to misdirect us, but I could have been wrong. What if we were being played? What if someone was out to take the Hobfield for himself and just when that was about to happen, Lazarov turns up?"

"It's a nice theory," Ruth said, "but we have no proof. No suspects either, come to that."

Calladine leafed through the case notes. There had to be something. "Darren Heap told his girlfriend Josie that Johnno Higgs would sort the new man out."

"Bravado on Johnno's part I'd say. He's not got the bottle," Rocco said.

"Is it worth speaking to Arran Hughes again, pressing him to tell us where the drugs he was found with came from?"

"I really don't think he knows," Rocco said.

Rocco was right. The lad was after making some quick money but had wimped out. Near the top of the mounting pile of paperwork was the latest report from Julian — his findings about the muddy boot print caught Calladine's eye. "What was Lazarov doing in Becca O'Brien's flat?"

"Hoping to sell her some dope?" Ruth suggested.

"She was dead, but there was mud on every floor in the place, the bedroom too." Calladine's eyes narrowed. Something had just occurred to him. "He was looking for someone but it wasn't Becca, he'll have seen straight away that she was dead. So why walk through every room? Who else did he expect to find in her flat?"

"No idea."

"The only other person living there, the one dossing down in the corner, was Johnno Higgs," Calladine said. He turned to Rocco. "Find him, and bring him in."

"You think Johnno shot Lazarov?" Ruth asked. "He's not got it in him, surely."

But Calladine was on the phone to Julian. "D'you have anything else that might help me find who killed Lazarov?"

"Lazarov's clothing is interesting," Julian said. "Dirty, as you might expect with someone living rough. His jacket was ripped in places. I think he may have been in a fight prior to his death. His knuckles are slightly grazed but there are no bruises on his face or body, so I'd say the other person came off worst."

"Thanks, that could be useful," Calladine said.

"What is even more useful is that we've done more work on Lazarov's clothing. We've found more of those black fibres on his jacket," Julian said. "Lazarov was a big man. Someone shorter than him swung a punch and missed his face, the fist only hit him in the chest."

"The same fibres as in Becca's flat?"

"Yes, Tom. I'd say they came from gloves. Find them and you have Lazarov's killer."

This was important evidence. Calladine looked towards Rocco's vacant desk. "Has he left?"

Ruth nodded. "He's trying the Hobfield first."

"Get a couple of uniforms to follow him. There might be trouble."

"We've spoken to Higgs a number of times," Ruth said. "I still don't see him shooting anyone."

"Perhaps he was scared," Calladine said. "Lazarov threatened him, and he saw his chance."

"What was he doing up at Gorse House in the first place?" she asked.

"I think he followed Lazarov up there. He knew it was him who was trying to take over and wanted to stop him. Sinclair told me he'd seen someone watching the workshop from the trees." Calladine checked his email. Julian had sent through the report on Lazarov's clothing and the fibres he'd found. "I'll pop along the corridor and bring Greco up to date," he said. "When Higgs is brought in, keep him happy until I'm ready for him."

CHAPTER 57

"This has got beyond a joke now," Johnno Higgs complained. "Why can't you pick on someone else for a change?"

"Calm down, Johnno, we just need to check a few things, ask a couple more questions, that's all," Calladine said.

Johnno looked a lot worse than the last time he'd been brought in. He was dishevelled and dirty, and the knuckles on both hands were bruised. "Hurt yourself?" Calladine asked. "You look like you've been in a fight."

"Fell, didn't I? I don't do fighting."

"What about shooting, Johnno? Do that, do you?" Johnno's eyes darted around. "Still dossing down in that flat in Heron House?"

"What of it?"

Calladine leaned towards him. "I need to know because I'm about to get a warrant to search it," he said. He turned to the desk sergeant. "Once he's processed, lock him up until I get back."

Calladine went back to the main office. Alice had already arranged the warrant, so they were good to go. "The place will be filthy," he warned Ruth. "We're looking for the gun, and those black gloves."

229

"I'll be surprised if we find them," she said.

"Don't be taken in, Ruth. Johnno Higgs is no loveable rogue. His knuckles are cut up and swollen, and he's got bruises on his face. I'd say he's been in a fight within the last few days."

"Someone like Higgs is a magnet for anyone on the Hobfield that fancies a barney," she said.

"Indulge me," Calladine said. "We don't find anything, we'll have to think again, but currently Johnno Higgs is our best bet."

It took only minutes to reach the Hobfield. Calladine parked directly outside the entrance to Heron House. A group of teenagers were hanging around, faces in their phones. Calladine glanced down the main corridor and saw one young lad banging on the door of Higgs's flat.

"The man's locked up," he said, moving the kid out of the way. They'd brought a uniformed officer with them, who battered the door down. Calladine and Ruth donned gloves and went inside.

The place was a dump. Johnno didn't have much and what he did have, mostly clothing, was heaped on an old mattress.

"Please tell me we don't have to rummage through that lot. Most of it's mucky, and it smells. Stuff's not seen a washing machine in weeks."

"Sorry, Ruth, we've no choice."

Ruth pulled a face but got on with it. "There could be wildlife living in this lot. I catch fleas and you're for it, Calladine. I'll make sure I pass 'em on."

But Calladine wasn't listening. He'd pulled the cushions off an old sofa and found a package hidden underneath. He unwrapped it. "Cocaine," he said. Worth a bit, too."

"We know he's dealing," Ruth said. "He told us."

"There's enough here to deal on an industrial scale. A bit ambitious for our Johnno."

Ruth found an old raincoat among the clothing. It looked clean, no mud or blood on it. She was about to toss it on to the pile of things she'd gone through when she felt something in the inside pockets. She pulled them out and held them up. "Black gloves. Covered in mud and what looks like dried blood."

"Good, but we still need the gun."

"I've gone through this lot, and there's certainly no gun."

Calladine went over and checked the mattress. It was intact, no holes or hiding places. He walked slowly around the rest of the flat. It was empty of furniture and there were no fitted cupboards. Nothing in the toilet cistern.

Ruth joined him. "The gloves and coke are real finds—"

"There is a gun, Ruth," he snapped. "And if it's here we need to find it."

"Don't get like that, it doesn't suit you. You're getting all stressed out again. I can tell, your colour changes, you've gone all grey in the face."

Ignoring her, Calladine walked into what would have been one of the two bedrooms. It was empty, its sparseness relieved only by a bright-red mat on the floor. He lifted one end with his toe. "The floorboards under here have been cut."

CHAPTER 58

Within the hour, Forensics were busy in Johnno's flat. Calladine had removed one of the cut floorboards and found a gun wrapped in an old T-shirt. Removing more of the boards, one of Julian's people also found an old pair of boots covered in mud and two mobile phones in a carrier bag. The footwear would have been what Higgs wore when he went up to Gorse House.

"We need to know if that's the gun that killed the two lads and Lazarov," Calladine told Julian. "The black gloves in that evidence bag — the fingers are badly frayed, hence the fibres you found. We need to know that they match, but given that," he nodded at the gun, "I suspect they will."

"We'll finish here and take everything back to the lab. I'll be in touch later on today," Julian said.

"Ruth," Calladine called. "We should get back, interview Johnno and see what he has to say for himself."

"Johnno Higgs played us," Ruth said. "All that talk about a small amount of dealing to keep himself in food and fags was nonsense."

"I'm wondering what else he's lied to us about," Calladine said.

"What d'you mean?"

"Becca O'Brien," he said. "He was in Heron House that night."

"Jade said he arrived at the flat after her," Ruth said.

"Yes, but who's to say it was his first visit of the night?"

"You think he might have killed Becca?" she asked.

"We have to consider the possibility."

* * *

When Calladine and Ruth went into the interview room, Johnno Higgs looked up and swore at them. "Whatever you think I've done, you can think again," he said. "I've already told you, I'm not into much these days."

Calladine sat down, placed a file of documents on the table and took out a photo. "I found this in your flat."

Higgs looked at the image of the package and shrugged. "Proves nowt."

"It's a small fortune in cocaine. Hardly not much. Where did you get it, Johnno?"

"Found it."

Calladine took a second photo from the file. This one showed the gun. "Did you find this too?"

Higgs looked rattled. "Look, it's not mine. I was hiding it for someone."

"Who?" Calladine asked.

"That foreign bloke, but he's dead now, so I stuffed it under the floorboards."

Calladine nodded. "We're running tests on the gun. We'll find out if it killed the two lads, but if we also discover it killed Lazarov — the 'foreign bloke' — that blows your story apart. He could hardly give you the thing if he was dead."

Johnno Higgs stared narrowly at Calladine. "Got a bloody answer for everything, 'aven't you?"

"You were at Gorse House. We know that because you were seen, but also your boots are covered in mud from there."

"How can you tell? What's so special about the mud in that place?"

"Forensically, quite a lot, Johnno, and we've found that same mud in a number of places you've been in recently."

The duty solicitor whispered something in Higgs's ear.

"He says I should tell you the truth," Higgs said.

"He's right," Calladine said. "You killed Lazarov, didn't you?"

Higgs nodded. "He threatened me, said if I didn't agree to work with him, he'd kill me. He hit me, too."

"You followed him to Gorse House?" Calladine asked.

"Yes. I tried to reason with him. I told him there was enough business round here for both of us, but he wouldn't listen. He went for me, fists flying." He rubbed his face. "I managed to dodge him — I'm smaller than him — but then he pulled a gun on me. I had to do something, or I'd have been dead."

"How did you get the gun off him?" Ruth asked.

"He pushed me against the wall, aiming the gun at me. I launched out with my fist. I only hit his chest, but it sent the gun spinning out of his hand and on to the floor. I was faster than him, I made a dive for the gun and shot him. Got him in the head, too. He went down like a stone. It was self-defence. I had to fight back, or he'd have killed me."

A jury might well agree with him. Lazarov was a dangerous villain and twice Higgs's size, and he did admit to pulling the trigger.

"The cocaine we found at yours was Lazarov's, wasn't it? You found it in the workshop and took it with you."

Higgs nodded. "

"Tell me about Becca O'Brien," Calladine said.

Higgs looked surprised. "What about her? Oh no, you're not pinning that one on me."

"We're still investigating, but we have found certain forensic similarities between the two cases."

Higgs turned to his solicitor. "What's he on about?"

"Your gloves," Calladine explained. "We're still checking but we believe that fibres from your black gloves were not only found on Lazarov's clothing but in Becca's flat too. Want to tell me about that?"

"Well, I was there, bound to have left some trace behind. But I didn't kill her," he insisted.

"Okay," Calladine said, "that'll do for now. But we'll talk again later."

"Can I go?"

"No. I don't think you appreciate how serious this is, Johnno. You are here on suspicion of murder. Certainly until we have the results of the forensic tests, you're staying with us."

CHAPTER 59

Calladine and Ruth returned to the main office, where Calladine asked Joyce to get him Roxy Atkins on the phone.

"What're you after?" Ruth asked.

"Whoever those two mobile phones belonged to — the ones found in Higgs's flat. I suspect one was Lazarov's and the other belonged to Becca O'Brien."

"You think Johnno killed her too?"

"Yes, Ruth, I do. Think about it."

Before he could explain, Joyce handed him the phone.

"The mobiles," Roxy said. "One was a burner PAYG, but I found a text in it, written in a foreign language. I had an interpreter look at it and it's Bulgarian, so I reckon that one belonged to Lazarov. The other was on contract to Becca O'Brien. The last call she made was to Johnno Higgs, on the night she died."

"Higgs took Becca's mobile," he told Ruth when the call finished. "Remember, it wasn't found in her flat, so it must have been taken before Jade arrived. It's in your interview notes from when you spoke to her."

"So what happened?"

"Johnno Higgs, that's what. I want this finishing," he said. "I'm going to ring Julian, see how he's doing with those fibres."

He went into his office to make the call. Minutes later he reappeared with a grin on his face. "Bingo. All the fibres are from Johnno's gloves, and Julian's testing the blood to see if it's Becca's. Let's go and have another chat with the man."

* * *

"You took Becca's mobile, Johnno. Why?" Calladine asked.

"I never. That's a lie," Higgs replied.

"We found it in your flat, hidden with the other things. So it's pointless denying it."

"She were dead, she didn't need it anymore."

"So you took it from her hand?" Higgs nodded. "Jade says she didn't have it when she was there. You told us that Jade arrived a few minutes before you. In light of what you've just said, that can't be right. Care to explain?"

"You're twisting things," Higgs said. "I can't remember what happened."

"In that case, I'll help you. You went to Becca's flat before Jade. Something happened between you and you ended up having a fight."

"No, no, you've got it wrong. I never harmed her."

"You said you didn't see the word 'sorry', or the image drawn in blood on the wall of Becca's flat."

"Because it wasn't there," Higgs said.

"You also said you'd no idea why the heating would be turned up so high."

He shook his head. "Becca couldn't pay the bills."

"We found black fibres from your gloves on the wall where the writing was. Plus a bloody thumb print you left when you scrawled the message. There were also fibres on the heating thermostat, again from your gloves, Johnno. What's the betting that when the blood on your gloves gets analysed, it turns out to be Becca's?"

Johnno Higgs now had a face like thunder.

"You saw Jade enter the flat and you followed her. She was upset, so you walked her to the bus stop, but then you went back a third time. You wrote that message and turned up the heat, hoping it would help the body decompose faster and so muddy the waters forensically."

Another whisper from his solicitor and Higgs finally lost it. He thumped the table in front of him.

"Stupid bitch wouldn't listen, would she? Kept going on about the foreign man and how she could get all the dope she needed for nowt if she told him where I was. He wanted me gone so he could have a clear run at that estate. Becca told him I was dossing at hers. We argued and she said yes, she'd dobbed me in. I was bloody mad. She'd told him everything, about my customers, the kids I use, the lot. I couldn't help myself after that. I saw red and laid into her with that wrench thing she kept behind the door in case of trouble. Next thing I knew, Becca wasn't moving anymore. She was bleeding on the floor, and I panicked."

"You're doing well, Johnno," Calladine said. "Carry on. How did you know to write the word 'sorry', and where did you get that image from?"

"Jade," he said at once.

"Jade said she was confused about the word. Had no idea why it was there or what it meant," Calladine said.

Higgs shook his head. "Can't help you with that one."

"I think you can. You see, I think you were trying to make Becca's murder look like that of Millie Reed all those years ago. You were hoping we'd pin it on Jade."

"That were down to Jade, not me."

"I doubt that. Jade was in no state to hurt anyone. She'd been hit on the head and was near collapse herself. You knew what had happened that day. Jade was hurt, and her mother was too drugged up to do anything about it."

"Becca wasn't much cop as a mother," Higgs said. "She was even worse back then. Why d'you think Jade was the way she was?"

"What happened, Johnno? When Jade told you about how Millie had attacked her, what did you do?"

"I wanted to help, make the Reed girl see that what she'd done was serious."

"You went up there, didn't you?" Calladine said.

"I didn't intend to do her any harm, but things got out of hand. We were in the kitchen — the granny was out feeding the chickens but she wouldn't have heard us anyway — the old bird was hard of hearing. That girl had a terrible temper. I mentioned Jade's name and she went berserk, went for me with a meat cleaver." He paused and looked at his solicitor, but the man was intent on his notes. "I had no choice. It were me or her. I picked up a heavy old rolling pin and whacked her across the head with it."

"The grandmother — is that when she had her stroke?" Calladine asked.

"Yes. She came back in, saw Millie lying in a pool of blood and dropped like a stone. I left her where she fell, and I hid the girl in that hole in the cellar where she was later found."

"You wrote 'sorry' on the boards you covered her with. Why?" Calladine said.

"I *was* sorry, Mr Calladine. It wasn't supposed to end like that. I felt for the girl, she didn't deserve all the aggro she got. All those years ago I just wanted to warn Millie off. I went up there and we argued, she wouldn't listen to reason. I didn't have anything against the kid. She was odd and the others in her class didn't like her, but she never bothered me."

"You did the same thing at Becca's, why?"

"Same reason. I didn't want to kill Becca either but she kept on and on about needing her fix. When I hit her there was no going back. I thought leaving the same word and picture behind would confuse you lot."

"It had precisely the opposite effect, Johnno. It linked the two cases."

Calladine picked up his notes and leaned back in the chair. They were done. Lazarov had killed the two lads but Johnno Higgs was responsible for the deaths of Millie Reed, Becca and Lazarov. For a man who'd always given the impression of being a mild-mannered, bumbling small-time dealer, that was some tally.

***

Calladine and Ruth returned to the main office. Greco was dealing with the charges against Marilyn and would also charge Sinclair with, among other things, perverting the course of justice.

Calladine told the others his good news. Case over, all of it. They had their man. Now Zoe could come home, and he could take a couple of days off, spend time with Kitty.

He was about to tell the others there'd be drinks in the Wheatsheaf on him later when he felt the familiar pain in his chest. This time it was no niggle. He gasped and gripped his arm. The last thing he saw before hitting the floor was Ruth looking down at him.

EPILOGUE

Ruth Bayliss walked out of Leesworth church and along the path into the graveyard. She stood in front of the two graves belonging to Freda and Frank Calladine. Beside it was one newly dug and covered in floral tributes. She bent down, picked up a card. *For a man well loved*, it read. How sad, and what a shame the flowers were getting bashed by the driving rain.

"You taking me home now?"

She swung round and nodded at the man sat on the bench. "Yep, I'm all done. The vicar is a darling. A couple of things to sort before the wedding and then we're ready for the off." She nodded at the new grave. "Who is he?"

"How should I know?" Tom Calladine replied.

"I presumed you'd have the plot next to your parents, it's been free all this time. I'm surprised you haven't got it bought and sorted before now."

"I'm in no hurry, believe me," he said getting to his feet.

"Come on then." She linked his arm.

"I'm not a bloody invalid you know. It was a scare, a bad angina attack that's all. I've got the pills, the diet sheet and Kitty bending my ear all the time. I don't want you harping on about death, that'll really finish me off."

"Fair comment. Zoe happy to be back?" she asked.

"Yes, but she and Jo liked it in Longnor, the peace and quiet appealed to them. Bit of a pipe dream at the moment, they've both got to work, but they've filed it under possibilities."

"You'd miss her terribly," she said.

"Might go with them. Can't carry on in the job for ever," Tom said.

"You don't mean that? You aren't seriously considering . . ."

Calladine started laughing. "Serves you right for all that talk of death, Bayliss. No, I'm not going anywhere."

"Good, cause I need a favour."

"I haven't got any money."

She thumped his arm, making him wince. "I want you to walk me down the aisle. My dad's dead and there's no one else I'd like to do it more than you."

There was a long silence. Calladine swallowed. "I'd love to," he said finally. I'm really touched that you've asked me. Are you sure? You don't have to ask me if you've got someone better."

"I want you, so shut it."

"Do I need a new suit?" he asked.

"Yep, and the trimmings, and you'll be giving a speech, so start practising."

"I've never given anyone away before. But I suppose if I have to start somewhere . . ."

He darted off ahead of her. He didn't fancy another thumping.

THE END

THE JOFFE BOOKS STORY

We began in 2014 when Jasper agreed to publish his mum's much-rejected romance novel and it became a bestseller.

Since then we've grown into the largest independent publisher in the UK. We're extremely proud to publish some of the very best writers in the world, including Joy Ellis, Faith Martin, Caro Ramsay, Helen Forrester, Simon Brett and Robert Goddard. Everyone at Joffe Books loves reading and we never forget that it all begins with the magic of an author telling a story.

We are proud to publish talented first-time authors, as well as established writers whose books we love introducing to a new generation of readers.

We won Trade Publisher of the Year at the Independent Publishing Awards in 2023 and Best Publisher Award in 2024 at the People's Book Prize. We have been shortlisted for Independent Publisher of the Year at the British Book Awards for the last five years, and were shortlisted for the Diversity and Inclusivity Award at the 2022 Independent Publishing Awards. In 2023 we were shortlisted for Publisher of the Year at the RNA Industry Awards, and in 2024 we were shortlisted at the CWA Daggers for the Best Crime and Mystery Publisher.

We built this company with your help, and we love to hear from you, so please email us about absolutely anything bookish at feedback@joffebooks.com.

If you want to receive free books every Friday and hear about all our new releases, join our mailing list here: www.joffebooks.com/freebooks.

And when you tell your friends about us, just remember: it's pronounced Joffe as in coffee or toffee!

www.ingramcontent.com/pod-product-compliance
Ingram Content Group UK Ltd.
Pitfield, Milton Keynes, MK11 3LW, UK
UKHW021436140325
4998UKWH00044B/746

9 781805 730378